IN PLAIN SIGHT

A DI SCOTT BAKER CRIME THRILLER

JAY NADAL

Published by Inkubator Books
www.inkubatorbooks.com

ISBN (eBook): 978-1-83756-076-9
ISBN (Paperback): 978-1-83756-077-6
ISBN (Hardcover): 978-1-83756-078-3

Previously published by the author as Captive.

PROLOGUE

The cold of the metal chilled her skin. Condensation raced down the sides of the metal box that held her. It was dark. Black. Blacker than coal. Hailey Bratton pushed harder against the sides, seeing the tiniest fleck of light above her. But her effort wasn't enough.

An overpowering stench assaulted her nostrils. An oily stench that brought tears to her eyes.

She desperately needed to pee. The more she tried to avoid thinking about it, the more her bladder spasmed its annoyance.

Her hands were numb; her palms pressed together had all but lost all feeling; the plastic tie cut into her wrists. Hailey wanted to scream, but the duct tape over her lips prevented her, allowing only the smallest of whimpers to escape. With her legs pulled into the foetal position, she tried to move, but every muscle hurt and ached from being cramped for so long. Each time she tried, she pushed against the sides of her prison. Each time her efforts were met with the immovable barrier that cocooned her.

She'd lost count of how many hours she'd been here. It

felt like days, but it had only been less than twenty-four hours. Time stood still as she waited, not knowing how long she'd be held prisoner, or when someone would come for her. Thoughts of dying a slow, painful death alone raced through her mind.

A throbbing pain banged in her head. Stress, dehydration, and panic all contributed to the symphonic sounds. She violently shook her body again, hoping that the box would move or her efforts would attract attention. She didn't know her location, but wherever it was, it was neither busy nor remote. The rumble of the odd car engine gave her hope, quickly followed by defeat as each sound faded into the distance.

Hailey hopelessly clawed at the sides. A new wave of panic washed over her. She needed to get out quickly before he came back.

How was another matter.

Her mind was a fog. Every time she breathed in, a musty, cloying, bitter odour enveloped her senses. A heavy mix of stale air, oil and sweat.

The sound of a metal door scraping along its runners shocked her back into the present. She froze. Was she finally going to be freed? Was a rescue imminent?

Her heart pounded against her chest. Her pulse throbbed in her temples. She frantically shook her body again and banged and thumped the soles of her bound feet against the end of the metal container. *Please help, help, I'm in here*, she recited over and over in time with her muffled screams.

Slow, steady footsteps grew louder. What felt like minutes elapsed between each step.

All her senses were on high alert as she heard the sound of a padlock springing open. An orb of light, like a white halo, crept in as someone gently lifted the lid. She screwed her eyes and pulled her hands up to shield her face when the light temporarily blinded her.

She cranked her head in a vain attempt to focus. As though this were a lunar eclipse, a dark figure cast a ghoulish shadow over her. An ice-cold bolt of fear sent shivers through her body when she finally saw. Her breathing grew rapid, her eyes fixed wide in terror.

This wasn't a rescuer at all.

The light bounced off the silver edge of the knife he held. Waves of nausea rippled through her as her belly heaved. She swallowed hard, sending the bile back down; the acidic taste stung and burnt her insides.

Hailey stared, paralysed with fear.

"I'M GOING to take good care of you. You're a precious commodity," said the figure as he gently wiped Hailey's flame red hair from her sweat-drenched brow.

He softly ran a finger down from her temple to her face. He followed the edge of her jaw down to her chin in a lover's caress. He savoured every sensation he felt through his finger.

"So beautiful, so delicate, like a china doll," he whispered as he licked his lips. His finger trembled in his anticipation and excitement.

"I have no idea why so many find redheads so unappealing. You're unique, a heavenly creation by the Lord Almighty. Sent to stand out from the crowd, and you, my dear, stand out. Oh, you certainly do with your pale skin, delectable curves and magnificent chest. My, oh my, you do look after yourself," he muttered as his eyes followed the curves of her ample breasts and the lines of her body.

For a long moment he paused, unable to continue, transfixed by her crotch.

He continued to observe. “It’s a nice touch.” He nodded as he ran a finger over her painted red toenails that matched her fingernails.

His eyelids flickered as he pulled in a sharp breath. His thoughts whisked him away on his own erotic journey.

He opened his eyes and glanced over at her strappy stilettos that lay neatly on his desk. His groin ached as he recalled the memory of seeing her wear them; the familiar click-clack sound had proved too much to bear.

He smiled as Hailey thrashed and squealed. She pulled her legs away from him, desperate to get away, which excited him further. A dark liquid crept from between her legs. Tears dripped from her scrunched-up eyes.

“Now, now, calm yourself. I want you to enjoy your time with me. You won’t need anyone else ever again.” He leant over her, pulled the tape away, and squeezed her mouth open with a firm grip of her cheeks.

He tipped a teaspoonful of white powder into the shallow opening her parted lips made. Hailey thrashed her head from side to side; a shrill scream emanated from deep within her.

“There, my dear, you need to rest now.”

Hailey gave one final thrash; then her world faded to black.

1

It didn't take long to remove all evidence of Hailey from Freddie's room. His brow furrowed in anger. His lips had tightened into a pencil-thin line; his jaw had locked tight, making his face ache. He hated Hailey and needed to remove every trace of her. From her cheap tacky New Look jeans that hung in his already overcrowded wardrobe, to her well-worn white trainers that sat at the end of his bed. He also hated her untidiness.

Anger wasn't a word he would use to describe how he felt about her. A seething, boiling rage fitted much better. She'd used him, bled him dry of money and had expected him to pay for everything.

Several of her surfer bracelets sat in a tangled pile by his bedside lamp. They were swiftly swept into a black bin liner that overflowed with every last trace of her. As he held her black stiletto shoes with the metal spiked four-inch heels, his mind momentarily flashed back to when he'd bought them. They'd been a gift for her to wear during the rampant sex session they'd had right there in his bed. She was good in bed, not great, just good. She'd at least worn the heels for him even if she'd turned down his request to act "filthy".

He glanced around the room, chest heaving from the resentment that flooded through him. *I want every damn thing gone.* Everything that reminded him of her. He hated Hailey's sickly, sweet voice, the smell of her Victoria's Secret body spray, and the tacky photographs he had pinned above his desk.

She didn't give a shit about him, so why should he waste another second thinking about her? *Fucking bitch.*

He'd start afresh, new everything. Right after he completely removed her from his life.

Freddie grabbed another black bin liner and proceeded to strip the linen from his bed. The pillowcases, the cream sheets and the pale blue duvet cover that she'd chosen. He'd hated them from the moment he'd seen them. She'd dragged him from the Asda superstore across to Matalan in Hollingbury.

Behind him were two black bin liners neatly tied up, the only evidence of their pathetic relationship. She'd used him. Women were all the same – it was always take, take, take.

Her scent assaulted his nostrils in every direction. It was like she still clung to him, desperate to leave her mark and determined to make sure he never forgot about her.

He blew air through his nose; then the obscenities followed, rolling off his tongue as he shook his head in frustration. "You'll never do this to anyone else again, you evil cow."

He'd spent what little money he had on her, or so she believed. A warm sense of satisfaction filled his belly. He had always pleaded poverty, only carrying a wallet with no more than a few tenners in the sleeve. He had deliberately left his Barclays bank statements lying around that showed a balance of no more than two hundred pounds. He'd noticed her taking a sneaky peek on several occasions. It was his Santander card that she never saw, kept hidden under one corner of the carpet. She never knew about the eye-popping five-figure balance that allowed him to enjoy his secret lifestyle.

Oh yes, he was certain Hailey had treated him like a mug, taken him for a fool. He had paid every time they went out. He had paid for the takeaways. He had paid for her shopping trips, the trips to the cinema and everything else she moaned about needing. His constant pleas of poverty had only fuelled her desire to bleed him dry.

Their time together had ended abruptly. She was gone, and he was glad of that. He would never have to listen to her moan ever again.

Freddie grabbed the Asda shopping bag that lay under his desk and pulled out a pack of bleach disinfectant wipes. Her scent still smothered him, stifling his airway and his space. He had hoped that an open window would have removed her presence.

Tearing the packet open with excitement, he then pulled out a few sheets and brought them up to his nose. He inhaled deeply, closing his eyes as the fresh, chemical fragrance soothed him. It cleansed his soul and took away his misery, her smell – and placated him.

He started with his desk, wiping down the surfaces in a methodical fashion. Slow, straight, and steady strokes in one direction gathered up a few flecks of dust and the odd strand of her hair. He discarded the wipes in a new bag before grabbing another fresh handful and systematically cleaning each table leg. Every few strokes would fuel his need to discard the wipes and replace them with fresh ones. He hated dirt; he hated filth. The room was contaminated, and she was the cause.

He didn't want to leave any traces behind. Sensing that

perhaps the six packets of bleach wipes wouldn't be enough, Freddie had gone back in and grabbed four bottles of Dettol spray, a pair of rubber gloves and a can of Glade air and fabric freshener – the crisp, white cotton fragrance his preferred choice.

His unusual purchase had attracted a brief cursory look from the store assistant. Her bold, garish green blouse struggled to contain her ample weight as she rocked from one foot to the other in boredom.

The smell of disinfectant bathed the room, sanitising it, much to Freddie's delight. His breath switched from slow and steady to rapid and shallow as he moved around his room. The idea that he had reclaimed his environment relaxed him as he moved on to the next possession or fixture. As he furiously wiped down smaller items, a mixture of anger and excitement raced through his veins. Nothing was left without disinfection. His bedside clock, books, mirror and each pen and pencil were meticulously sanitised.

He had only just begun, but his work would take the next few hours. Once he was satisfied that he had covered every square inch of his room, he would start again from the beginning. His room needed a deep clean, and he would stay up all night if necessary to get the job done to his satisfaction.

Freddie didn't care about her now. She was gone.

"What goes around comes around," he muttered quietly as he cleaned. "Good riddance, you stupid bitch."

2

The team gathered around the incident board and looked at the picture pinned to it of a young woman. "This is Hailey Bratton. She's been missing since last night, and there are concerns for her safety," Scott announced as he crossed his arms.

Mike raised a brow. "There's nothing unusual in that, guv. How many times have we heard of a person going missing, only to find the person returns as if nothing's happened?"

He had a point. Missing people was nothing new. More than two hundred and fifty thousand people went missing in the UK every year. The county of Sussex had an average of more than ten thousand people go missing annually. With the thin blue line becoming even thinner each year because of budgetary cuts, the police had neither the time nor the resources to investigate many of the cases. Many children's homes in Sussex accounted for a high volume of runaways. As the team had found on their recent child trafficking case, it was a vile issue that pushed out its tentacles to all corners of the UK.

Scott nodded in agreement. "That's a fair point, Mike. I've lost count of the number of times we've been sent on a wild goose chase, but a missing person is still a missing person. There are genuine concerns for her safety. So we still need to do a risk assessment." He unscrewed the cap on his water bottle and took a glug to satisfy his parched throat. "The reason this case has been elevated to us from uniform is because Hailey is a student at the University of Sussex."

"What's been done by the university so far?" Raj asked without lifting his gaze from the rich tea biscuit he was dunking into his tea. He was timing it to the millisecond. If he immersed it too long, the biscuit would break off and disappear into his brew.

"As much as could be done," Scott replied. "The university increased security patrols, but with a campus that size, the coverage is still relatively thin. Uniform have been on campus doing regular patrols and are making the usual enquiries but have drawn a blank." Scott tapped Hailey's picture with the end of his pen. "It's because this lady has gone missing and possibly come to harm that this case has been referred to us."

"What do we know about her already, guv?" asked Abby.

"Not a lot. A popular student studying history and politics. No run-ins or priors, and according to reports from uniform, her disappearance is out of character for her. She was reported missing by her flatmate. They share a student house on Upper Lewes Road. Her boyfriend has confirmed that he hasn't seen her either. So, Abby, she is currently low to medium, but can you do a risk assessment for me?"

"Fallen in with a bad crowd, drugs maybe?" Abby asked.

Scott shook his head. "Uniform didn't uncover anything to suggest that, but that's what we need to find out."

Scott grabbed his whiteboard marker and started to make a few notes of key tasks around Hailey's picture.

"Okay, team," Scott said. He paused for a moment and stared at the floor. In his heart, there was an uncomfortable awkwardness around using the word 'team', especially after the tragic loss of Sian during their last case. They all felt a pain that was still fresh in the minds of those gathered.

Scott lifted his chest as he inhaled deeply. "Raj, can you contact Hailey's parents, get the background on her? Find out how often she's been in contact with them recently. Was anything bothering her that she may have told them?"

"I'm on it. I'll also contact the faculty and the university counselling services to see if they can help. I'll find out who her friends are so we can build a better picture of her and get a timeline of her last known movements."

Scott nodded his approval and gave Raj one thumb up. He was pleasantly surprised with Raj's plan of action. Usually, Raj required a push to get him on the right track of thinking.

Perhaps in the light of Sian's death, he's being more conscientious.

Scott added, "You might want to find out which phone provider she was using." Raj scribbled on his notepad. "See if you can organise a triangulation to identify the last known point where her phone was used."

Raj raised his pen in agreement.

Scott said, "Abby and I will go and have a chat with her boyfriend. Mike, I know it's a big job, but can you liaise with the campus security team and review any CCTV footage? There might be a chance she was spotted in the last twenty-four hours. Get a PC to help you. I'm sure it's already been done, but we need to be sure as a team that we've covered every angle. Take Raj with you and interview her flatmate. Check the usual things like email accounts and social media."

Mike added that to his notes and gave Scott the thumbs up.

"Whilst you're there, Mike, can you bag up her toothbrush and her pillowcase in case we need DNA samples?"

"Will do, guv."

"Any further questions?" Scott offered.

Mike, Raj, and Abby gave a collective shake of their heads before getting up and returning to their desks.

A stab of pain hit Scott in the chest as he watched them wander off. He needed to keep the team going, they all had a job to do, and that was to serve the public. He knew deep down that the team was struggling. Sian had been a junior member of the team, only recently starting her career in CID. Abby had taken Sian under her wing on more than one occasion to support and guide Sian as her skip.

Despite his own personal and professional pain, Scott knew he had to dig deep and rely on his leadership.

The internal investigation into the Edmunston-Hunt School case had already begun within hours of its tragic conclusion. It would no doubt rumble on for quite some time. The early findings had exonerated Scott; however, it had been noted that a weakness in the chain of command meant lessons needed to be learnt. Chief Constable Lennon supported the recommendation that stronger accounting and risk assessments needed to be done for all officers across the county.

Scott knew that the job carried risks. Every case, every visit to make enquiries, every surveillance job, even every arrest carried inherent risks for all officers. But he still took Sian's death personally. She'd been a member of his team – the newest member who had perhaps needed closer supervision. Since her death, he had put himself in Sian's situation and thought about whether the outcome would have been the same. Could *he* have fought off Sanders? Would she still be here if she'd gone in there with backup? Had they missed the clues earlier in the investigation?

These were the questions that rolled around inside his head each day. He owed it to the team and to Sian to keep pushing through every day.

3

Scott sat down heavily in his office chair and stared into space. The day had just begun, but his body felt weary. His mind felt tired, and his thoughts were all over the place. The last few weeks had ranked as being some of the most challenging he'd ever experienced.

But one thing for certain was the sheer brilliance and resolve of the team that he had the pleasure of managing. The whole team, including himself, had been offered counselling in the wake of Sian's death. Detective Superintendent Meadows had gone to great lengths to encourage both Abby and Scott to take up the offer. Both had declined.

Scott knew that Abby had been deeply traumatised by the last few moments that she'd spent with Sian. She'd been quiet and withdrawn in the days after the attack. A deeply private person, Abby had refused to seek help or acknowledge the grief, instead choosing to block it out and push on.

Scott leant back, the chair creaking underneath his weight, as his mind drifted back to Sian's funeral. That day had proved to be a particularly challenging time for the team and the force itself. Chief Constable Lennon had led the tributes with a heartfelt speech that touched on Sian's career within the force. He'd spoken at great length about her talent and her traits of diligence, perseverance, and thoroughness, which had made her a popular and well-respected officer.

An eerie silence enveloped the church as Lennon spoke. His authoritative yet compassionate words were punctured by intermittent sobs from those gathered. Abby, Mike, and Raj sat together for support. Scott sat alongside Cara, his hand in hers. As they occasionally exchanged sad glances, a quick and reassuring rub of his hand with her thumb was the only gesture of support she could offer. The heavy weight of responsibility stifled Scott. A heady mixture of emotions threatened to engulf him as a deep sense of guilt pulled him into the darkened abyss.

The service itself had nevertheless been an opportunity to rejoice in her life and to remember the vivacious, funny, and kind soul that Sian was.

Jerry and Tricia Mason, Sian's parents, sat on the front pew, transfixed on her coffin. Throughout the service, Jerry had his arm around his wife, who often dabbed her eyes with a tissue. Jerry momentarily left her side to stand at the front and pay tribute to his daughter. He stood behind the lectern and pulled out a sheet of paper from the inside of his jacket before placing his glasses on the tip of his nose. He spoke the words no parent should ever have to say. It was something Scott knew only too well, having lost his own daughter, Becky, in a tragic hit and run.

His hand trembled as he tried to keep his composure, voice faltering. Those gathered listened quietly. Some smiled, some nodded, and others were moved to tears. He talked about the day that, as proud parents, they had watched their daughter graduate from police training college. Jerry recalled how she'd stood there in her immaculate police uniform, and even though she was a grown woman, she was still his little girl.

Cara tightened her grip of Scott's hand as tears chased each other down her cheeks.

Sian's best friend from university recalled their carefree days in Nottingham, and how she secretly loved to be wild and occasionally daring. But as she elaborated, Sian's definition of daring was quite tame in comparison to others. She recalled the time that they were driving down the road, and Sian proceeded to wind down the window and shout out, "I've got no knickers on." A crackle of laughter and a few claps echoed around the ancient walls of the church and offered a rare moment of light-heartedness.

It was an uncomfortable and deeply personal moment for Scott when he came face-to-face with Jerry and Tricia Mason. Despite offering his sympathies, anything he said seemed completely inadequate in that moment. Sensing Scott's unease, Jerry had given him a reassuring squeeze on the arm, and Tricia had given him a warm hug as she whispered, "Thank you," in his ear. It was a humbling moment, and Scott immediately understood that Sian's wonderful qualities had come from her parents.

As they filed out after the service, Scott saw his former boss DCI Jane Harvey. She had slipped into the church at the last minute and found an empty space at the back. Despite her forced early retirement, her unrivalled loyalty to her team was clear to Scott with her attendance.

Harvey was the first of many to make their way to Sian's parents to offer condolences. She declined the offer of attending the wake. Her presence probably hadn't gone down too well with Chief Constable Lennon or Detective Superintendent Meadows.

Shaking the regretful memories from his mind, Scott stood up and threw on his jacket. The next few days and weeks would no doubt be a challenging time for his team. Everything they did from now on would be closely watched and scrutinised. For this reason alone, he needed to make sure everything was done by the book.

He left his office, en route to brief DSI Meadows.

4

Scott announced himself at Meadows's office with a double tap on the open door. Meadows briefly glanced up; his pen hovered over the paper, his writing interrupted.

Meadows gave him his usual small insincere smile. Scott hated it.

"Come in, Scott. What can I do for you?" Meadows asked as he leant back in his chair. He nodded for him to sit, then began adjusting his blue and red striped tie.

Meadows was always immaculately dressed. His dark charcoal grey two-button suit was always either accompanied by a white or pale blue shirt as standard. His ties were either dark red or blue and red horizontally striped.

Scott had often thought that Meadows had an uncanny resemblance to the US comedian and TV presenter Jon Stuart when he was in his forties. High forehead with a full head of short, grey hair. They might have looked similar, but Meadows lacked the satirical wit, charm, and enigmatic appeal that Stuart boasted.

"How is the team holding up?" Meadows asked as he interlocked his fingers and placed them on the desk.

It didn't pass Scott's notice that Meadows had referred to 'the team', as opposed to 'you and the team'.

"They are holding up well, sir. It's still early days, and it's still fresh in *all* our minds, but I'm there to support them. We're going to be busy with this new investigation."

Meadows raised a brow. "Well, we need to reassure the team that we're here to support all of them in any way we can."

There he goes again saying 'the team'...

Scott spent the next few minutes providing a brief outline of their new case.

"Any leads in the investigation?" Meadows asked.

"Not yet, sir. The case has only just been referred to us, and we've just had our first meeting. I'm sending Raj and Mike out to visit her student digs, and Abby and I are off to have a chat with her boyfriend."

"Okay, well, keep me informed. I don't need to remind you that the force is reeling from DC Mason's death. There are a lot of extra eyes watching this station *and* the conduct of our officers, so I don't want any heroics, understood?"

Scott clenched his teeth. There were never any heroics, as Meadows put it, and the unnecessary implication only annoyed Scott. He said nothing, knowing that if he opened his mouth, he'd probably regret his words.

Meadows leant forward, fixing his stare on Scott, as if to emphasise the importance of what he was about to say. "Scott, you may have been cleared of misconduct, but questions have been raised about your methods of leadership. I hasten to add that it's not me who raised questions." Meadows held his hands up, as if to show disappointment.

I bet you didn't.

Meadows readjusted his tie once again. "And I imagine it's

probably the reason your name hasn't come up as a possible replacement for DCI Harvey in either an acting or permanent capacity. I think your job now is to vindicate your position and to continue building on your good work as an inspector."

Talk about giving me a slap with two hands, you hypocritical bastard.

"Anyway, we're fortunate enough to get your team back up to a full complement, as we have a new DC starting. A Detective –" Meadows searched through the paperwork on his desk before pulling out a sheet. "Detective Constable Helen Swift. Thirty, comes with good experience, and joins us from Cambridgeshire."

Scott was taken aback by the news. "I was unaware the final decision had been taken following the recent interviews, sir."

Meadows looked perplexed. "Perhaps DCI Harvey had forgotten to pass on the information to you. There were a lot of things that DCI Harvey wasn't doing, and perhaps this was an oversight on her part."

Scott wasn't happy about how Meadows was questioning DCI Harvey's integrity, especially considering she wasn't here to defend herself.

"DC Swift should be with us tomorrow morning, so show her around and make her feel welcome. I'll leave it in your capable hands to get her up to speed on the current case. Any questions?" Meadows raised an eyebrow. "If not, then close the door on your way out."

"No, sir," Scott replied as he got up and left the room.

I would ask why you're such an arsehole, but you'd probably take that as a compliment.

5

"We've got a new DC joining us tomorrow," Scott remarked as he drove himself and Abby on the Lewes Road out of Brighton towards the University of Sussex campus.

Abby was watching the suburban sprawl of Brighton thin out as they headed north-east out of town.

"I thought the decision hadn't been made yet?" Abby said, surprise lacing her tone.

Scott shrugged. "That's what I thought, too, but Meadows just sprang it on me. One of the officers we interviewed will be joining us, DC Helen Swift."

"Hmm...she was the one from Cambridge?" Abby asked.

"Yep, that's the one."

"How do you think she'll fit in after...?" Abby trailed off.

There was an uncomfortable pause as they were reminded of Sian.

"Only time will tell," Scott said. "It would be all too easy to keep comparing the new DC to Sian, but that wouldn't be fair on either of them. At the end of the day, the new DC is starting a job with a new force. It's just a shame that she is joining under slightly difficult circumstances."

Within minutes Scott was following the signs for the University of Sussex campus. The hustle and bustle of Brighton was replaced with a serene, wooded landscape.

The sprawling campus of the university was set beside Stanmer Park, with beautiful woodland walks and extensive open lands offering the perfect haven for wildlife and people alike. It was a popular spot for families to spend lazy afternoons enjoying a picnic and for walkers to enjoy wooded trails. Stanmer Park blended seamlessly into the wooded landscape that stretched beyond that was part of the South Downs National Park. For all intents and purposes, anyone could have been mistaken for thinking they were miles from the nearest civilisation.

"It's been a while since I was last here, as a student. So much has changed with the expansion of new, modern teaching buildings and accommodation," Scott remarked. "All the nights I spent at the East Slope bar drinking snakebite and black. The bar isn't even here now," he added, looking around.

Abby laughed. "Now you're showing your age... Snakebite and black?"

"Yep, and that was tame. I wasn't brave enough to try the brain neutraliser."

"I can't imagine you drunk," Abby said, looking at Scott through narrowed eyes.

"No, not me, I was a good boy," Scott said, his expression as deadpan as possible.

"It's just so nice round here. I'd love to run through these wooded trails," Abby said, her gaze fixed on the wooded area beyond the slope.

Scott parked up in one of the many car parks scattered

around the campus. They followed the signs on foot towards the East Slope accommodation blocks.

Scott observed students milling around and chatting, others walking from one block to another. With the end of term fast approaching, there were decidedly fewer students, as many had finished their exams and left for the holidays.

The familiar single-storey building that was the East Slope bar had been replaced with an impressive three-storey student information hub that housed an optician's, a pharmacy, a café, and a shop. They followed the brick path that ran alongside one of the accommodation blocks. Foliage from the mature trees left a mottled patchwork of light and dark as the sun crept through gaps in the canopy.

The East Slope accommodation took Scott's breath away. Twelve rows of flat-roofed single-storey accommodations, which once staggered up the hillside, had been bulldozed and replaced with clusters of three-storey, stylish blocks, with beige brickwork, modern facilities and cycle racks.

Abby pinched her nose and sniffed as they entered, whilst staring at Scott. "Hardly a clean fresh bouquet..."

"Smells like a mixture of stale sweat, booze, dirty clothing and weed," Scott said. "Yep, welcome to student land." He gave a jaunty wink.

The block and room number they needed belonged to Hailey's boyfriend. Scott knocked twice on the door and waited a few moments before he knocked again, more firmly. It shook in its frame.

A young man with dark brown eyes opened the door just a few inches. He looked suspiciously at them.

"We are looking for Freddie Coltrane," Scott enquired.

The young man looked between Abby and Scott. "Um, who's asking?"

"I'm Detective Inspector Baker, and this is my colleague

Detective Sergeant Trent from Brighton CID," Scott announced as they both held up their warrant cards.

"Are you Freddie?" Scott asked.

The man paused, clearly weighing up his options before nodding.

"May we come in? We'd like to ask you a few questions about Hailey Bratton."

Freddie Coltrane was dressed in dark blue jeans, a white T-shirt, and a crease-free light blue denim shirt. His neatly gelled brown hair and designer stubble suggested that personal appearance was high on his list of priorities.

He stood to one side to allow the officers to enter. With the three of them in the room, space suddenly became tight. The room was just wide enough to fit a single bed widthways along one end beneath the window. To the left was a desk and a double wardrobe, and to the right was a small bedside table. Two paces forward and he'd be touching Freddie's bed.

The three of them stood in the only space available. It was a dark and gloomy room, but surprisingly clean, uncluttered, and tidy. A hint of bleach hung in the air.

Scott and Abby exchanged a glance.

Freddie crossed his arms defiantly over his chest. "What can I do for you?"

"We'd just like to ask you a few questions about the recent disappearance of Hailey Bratton."

Freddie nodded as Abby pulled out her notepad and pen, ready to start taking notes.

"We understand you are in a relationship with Hailey. Is that correct?" Scott said.

"Yeah."

"And when did you last see her?"

Scott noticed Freddie's eyes shift down to his left, which suggested that there was an internal conversation going on.

Freddie's eyes then tracked up to the right, which Scott took as a cue Freddie was about to lie.

"A couple of days ago, I guess. She was over here and spent the night with me."

"Can anyone confirm that?" Scott pushed.

Freddie shrugged. "Dunno. Why? You think I had something to do with it?"

"I'm not suggesting anything, Freddie. We just need to corroborate your story and will be asking the same questions of everyone who knows her. And what was your relationship like?"

He laughed. "I'd hardly call it a relationship. It's just a bit of fun, you know, the stuff you do at university. It's not like we were getting married tomorrow, eh?"

Scott's lack of response left an uneasy feeling in the room.

Freddie was keen to fill it. "We liked a good drink, got pissed up and grabbed a burger. Most of the time we came back here and you know..."

Scott shook his head. "You know what?"

Freddie narrowed his eyes and looked between Abby and Scott. A hint of embarrassment tinged his cheeks. "Seriously...Do I really need to say?"

"It would be helpful, Freddie, because DS Trent is taking notes."

Freddie sighed and stuffed his hands in his pockets. "We'd come back here and have sex for a few hours. There... you satisfied?"

Abby interjected, "Have you any idea as to why she may have gone missing?"

Freddie shook his head. "No, none."

"Did she say anything to suggest that something was bothering her, or that she was in trouble?"

There was another slight shake of the head from Freddie.

Abby continued, "Any idea where she may have gone, or do you know of any other friends or family close by?"

"No, I haven't got a clue."

Scott noticed a pack of bleach wipes sitting on the shelf above his desk. "I have to say, Freddie, this is probably the cleanest, tidiest, and freshest-smelling student room I've ever been in. I'm impressed."

Scott's observation appeared to unnerve Freddie. "I don't like a mess. Mum always said a tidy room is a tidy mind."

Scott felt Freddie probably took that advice to the extreme, as he noticed four pencils neatly aligned on the desk and several pairs of trainers and boots in a neat row beneath the desk. He noticed through the partially open wardrobe door that his clothes were neatly organised by colour.

Abby tapped her pen on her notepad. "Well, Freddie, we'll continue to make our enquiries over the next day or so and may need to come back to ask you further questions. Will you be around?"

Freddie nodded quickly. "And when you find her, remind her that she owes me thirty quid. She's pissed me off by disappearing with my money. No trace of her, bloody typical."

His outburst surprised the officers.

Scott said, "Are you suggesting that the thing bothering you most about her disappearance is the fact she owes you money?"

"Hey, listen. Thirty quid is a lot of money for a student. She is always borrowing money off me, and I never get a single penny back. The one time I do ask, she disappears. Cheeky mare."

They left Freddie and headed outside. Scott and Abby paused by the East Slope bar, and Abby glanced back up to the halls they had just left.

Her eyes narrowed. "You know, for someone whose girlfriend is missing, he didn't seem particularly concerned about her safety or her whereabouts. He seemed more annoyed about his money than anything else."

Scott stood there with his hands in his pockets. "He knows more than he's letting on."

6

The man sat back in his chair and closed his eyes, his feet, crossed at the ankles, resting on the edge of the desk. Random songs that were being played on his favourite radio station, Smooth Radio, satiated his mind. His little DAB radio sat alongside his laptop. The only other two things on his desk were a glass of red wine and a small desktop lamp that cast a faint glow across the room.

His fingers tapped in rhythm to a song by the Four Seasons. A small smile broke on his face, pleased with his ability to tap in time with the beats of the song.

As much as he liked Smooth Radio, he found their adverts frustrating, which always spoilt the ambience. The Four Seasons segued into 'Dreams' by Fleetwood Mac.

Ah, one of my favourites.

His enjoyment was cut short when the song faded out early to make way for an advert from some garage that he didn't quite catch the name of.

Who cares if you've been servicing Mercedes for thirty years? Why don't you just piss off?

He glanced at a long rectangular metal box that sat on the

far side of the room. The thought of opening the lid sent dark, erotic shivers through him. It never failed to surprise him just how excited he got each time he lifted the lid to stare at his prize. He felt like a child on Christmas Day opening his presents, a mixture of curiosity and excitement rippling through him at the prospect of what he might find.

He slowly rose from his chair. "Well, you're desperate to be free... I think we're done with you, and you're ready to go."

As he knelt by the box, his fingers quivered with anticipation. He released the padlock from its housing.

He lifted the lid and took in an exquisite soft breath before releasing it. "Look, Sally, Hailey's still fast asleep. She's clearly enjoying staying with us, don't you think? Yes, I thought you'd agree."

His eyes opened wide in excitement as he examined Hailey. "You are just so beautiful. Simply divine and a gift from the gods. I'm so thankful that our paths crossed. Thankfully the police didn't come to your rescue. They were clearly far more stupid than I expected them to be. And now the time has come for us to say our goodbyes. You see, our relationship was a brief one, and if I'm honest, my wife, Sally, doesn't want me to have anything too permanent."

He reached out to caress Hailey's face but paused a moment before touching her.

"You've been so comfortable here. You haven't had the opportunity to meet her, but I know she approves of you. She told me not so long ago."

At the end of his tenderly spoken words, he pulled out a small pair of scissors from his pocket and cut off one of her curls. He delicately folded it, then placed it in a small heart-shaped silver pendant box.

He sat back on his haunches to take one final moment to admire this beauty in front of him. "Thank you for my little present. I shall cherish it forever," he said softly. "But for now, my sweet princess, you need to rest."

He reached in and tried to pull Hailey up, lifting her from under her armpits. Getting her out of the box proved more of a challenge than he'd anticipated. Every time he tried to lift a section of her body, her weight was redistributed elsewhere. He hadn't factored in that moving an unconscious dead weight was considerably harder than moving someone who was conscious. After several failed attempts, he gave up.

Then an idea came to him.

He walked round to the back of the metal container and with all his strength got a firm hold beneath the box. He tipped it over to one side, forcing Hailey to spill out.

"That's much better," he said through short, sharp breaths.

He grabbed her by the wrists and dragged her across the floor, each step straining his muscles. Once she was propped up into a seated position, he bear hugged Hailey from behind and used every ounce of strength to lift her. His teeth clenched under the exertion.

He blew out a laboured breath after he finally managed to dump her in the boot of his car.

He took a moment to catch his breath, focusing hard on the darkness of the night. There was no one around, no curious bystanders, no workers, or any late-night revellers.

"I told you, Sally, that I didn't need any help. They'd just try to control me like everyone else has. The doctors, the institutions, and the system. It was always about controlling me. You see, I'm too clever for them. Besides, with you by my side, what more could I want?"

With a turn of the key, he started his car and drove off slowly into the darkness.

He'd chosen his spot carefully. No one would disturb

them there, nor would anyone find Hailey until the morning at the earliest.

She shifted and moaned; her semi-conscious state gave him greater ease of movement as he manoeuvred her between two trees. Her muffled groans were quiet enough to not disturb him. Her eyes occasionally fluttered open beneath her sweaty, lank hair that clung to her pasty face.

He smiled to himself, pleased with his impeccable timing. Hopefully, she'd be awake soon to see his parting gift.

The undergrowth and surrounding hedges rustled in the cool summer night's air. Nocturnal creatures rummaging for food and hunting under the darkness of the night would be his unsuspecting audience.

He secured a length of rope around each of her wrists before securing them separately to two trees. Supporting her waist, he got her to stand. Her legs flailed as she fought to take control. With his other hand, he pulled the two supporting ropes tight, stringing her up in a crude crucifix position that forced her head to flop forward.

He took a few steps back to admire his handiwork, pleased with what he'd been able to achieve so far. Pulling a sharp knife from his back pocket, he leant forward and nicked the skin on her neck. The strike caused a gagged Hailey to squeal. Her eyes shot wide open.

The moon's glow in the clear night sky and the torch that he'd left close by were enough to illuminate the shiny beads of blood that formed on her neck. They seemed to merge magnetically to form a trickle that crept down her neck.

Hailey hung dazed, her eyes flickering.

A deep grumble emanated deep from within her attacker's throat. Then he inhaled deeply and leaned in closer. Hailey bucked for a moment as he came within touching distance of her. He licked her, and the warm metallic taste of her blood sent shivers through his body; his eyes rolled back as he savoured the flavour on his tongue.

This is just the beginning.

"Bless you, Hailey. I admire your courage; perhaps that's why I chose you. But now you're free to go." He drew the knife across her neck. The sharp steel sank deeply into her soft flesh.

He stepped back briefly to admire his handiwork as pulses of dark liquid erupted from her neck.

Hailey choked, her eyes widening more. For a brief moment, her head flailed around like a woman possessed before dropping one final time in exhaustion.

He stepped in closer and ran his fingers through the warm blood as it pulsed over his hand. He rubbed the viscous fluid between his fingers before licking the tip of his thumb, savouring the sweet stickiness as it clung to the insides of his cheeks.

"Oh, you're good. You're really good. I knew I could trust Sally to find the right person," he said, smiling. He tilted his head as he studied Hailey with curiosity.

With his knife firmly in his grip, he ran the thin blade deep across her navel like a butcher would with a thick cut of meat. More blood trickled as he thrust one hand into the open wound. He savoured the warm feel of her innards as they enveloped his limb.

With a thrust, he pulled out part of her intestines and left them hanging through the open wound. She jerked frantically for just a few seconds before she succumbed.

Hailey's arms took her full weight as her head slumped forward one last time.

7

The morning sun warmed Scott's face as he ran along the seafront. It sat high in the blue sky as seagulls drifted in the thermals along the shoreline, their familiar screeches signalling their presence. The hustle and bustle of Brighton played out around him. The familiar line of traffic snaked its way along the seafront, starting and stopping at the multitude of traffic lights that dotted the road.

On this occasion Scott had chosen not to listen to his iPhone as he ran, choosing instead to soak up the sounds of life around him. He was already two miles into his run, but his body struggled to keep up the pace. His mind drifted, as it invariably did whenever he ran. Work was preoccupying his mind too much. In recent weeks, it had been the only thing that he thought about.

A pang of guilt twisted inside his chest. He'd been so busy at work that he hadn't taken the time to visit Tina's and Becky's graves. He knew that he was coping better without his wife and child. He didn't have this overwhelming urge to break down and cry. He would never fully come to terms with their deaths, but acceptance was a far better state of mind than daily grief, sadness, and guilt.

He made a promise to himself to visit them at the earliest opportunity.

Scott always regarded himself as a strong person, able to face extreme pressures whilst maintaining a level head. However, he had to admit that he hadn't handled things well over recent weeks. Sian's death had affected him. It was the first time he'd ever experienced losing a member of his team in that way, and more importantly someone under his command.

I've got to pull my socks up and get a grip of the situation. My team needs me to be their backbone.

He wiped the sweat from his brow with the back of his hand. He was better than this, he knew that. He had amazing support; Cara was *his* backbone.

As he approached Hove, he saw Abby a few yards ahead stretching and limbering up against railings.

"You took your time, old man," she said, grinning at him.

"Maybe so, but if you keep stretching like that, you'll end up in A & E."

"Scott Baker, what you fail to realise is that you're a few years older than me, and women are just naturally more flexible than men. I reckon you have the problem, not me."

Scott pushed Abby playfully as they made their way down the steps to the beach. Their feet sank into the pebbles, which made walking anything but graceful.

Abby unfolded the TRX and fixed it to an anchor point on the green weathered railings that separated the beach from the promenade. Scott and Abby were both keen TRX enthusiasts and enjoyed exercising outdoors with the smell of the sea air, the sound of the seagulls, and busy Brighton life passing them by.

They took turns going through some basic stretching

exercises. Following his run, sweat was already dripping from Scott's pores. The TRX fast drained his remaining energy. Abby, on the other hand, didn't appear out of breath as she aggressively puffed away through each exercise when it was her turn, enjoying the challenge and demands that she placed on her body. Any exercise was like a drug to Abby. It cleared her mind; it melted away her stresses and helped her to forget about the world around her for those few brief moments.

Passing her the handles, Scott asked, "Did you do much last night?"

Abby began doing back rows as she anchored her feet against the sea wall. With her eyes firmly fixed on the railings above her, she appeared reluctant to say much.

Then she said, "I stayed at Jonathon's last night, and don't you say a word."

"You dirty stop-out...I didn't think you had it in you," teased Scott.

"Give it a rest. Anyone would think I'm Mother Theresa the way you talk about me."

"Well, it was only a few weeks ago that you were spraying on perfume, and now you're playing tonsil tennis under the duvet."

"Seriously, Scott, you have a one-track mind. I seriously don't know what Cara sees in you. Besides, it wasn't Brut. It was Sexy Amber from Michael Kors."

"Check you out, Sexy Amber...You sure it wasn't Sexy Abby?" He laughed.

Abby shook her head in resignation. "You wait till I speak to Cara. I'm going to get the gossip on you. Then we'll see who's laughing."

Scott held his hands up in resignation. "I'm just joshing you. You're so easy to wind up."

Abby held up her hand. "No, it's fine. If you want to play

dirty, then game on. This is war," she said, pretend snarling at him.

"In all seriousness, all joking apart, I'm glad you're happy. If he makes you happy and breaks your barren spell, then that's great."

"O, less of the barren! I wasn't gagging for it or anything. Yes, he does make me happy, and we are having a good laugh. And it's easy. Rottingdean isn't far away. He hasn't got any kids to worry about. My kids are getting old enough to stay with their gran without any fuss. He's an attractive fella, so yes, naturally, I fancy him."

Scott heard the sincerity in Abby's words and was pleased for her.

He grabbed the TRX handles and did some triceps extensions. His eyes focused on the horizon where the clear blue sky met the shimmering sea. His eyes tracked the multitude of yachts and sailing boats that departed Brighton Marina daily. The calm, clear conditions made it perfect sailing weather.

Abby took a long slug from her water bottle. "Is Meadows still giving you a hard time?"

"Pretty much," Scott said through heavy grunts and a grimace. "But nothing I can't handle."

Abby raised an eyebrow in suspicion when Scott briefly glanced in her direction. "Now tell the truth."

Scott paused in his exercise. "I get the feeling he's hoping I'll crack or slip up. He's already insinuated I'm not chief inspector material, and that I need more time 'in the trenches'."

"That's a bit harsh."

"Possibly, but I just think he's flexing his muscles."

"I don't think you two will ever get on."

"You're probably right. He's got his own agenda. DCI Harvey didn't fit into that agenda, and perhaps I don't either.

He's very much a yes-man, and even though I don't like to talk out of turn regarding a senior officer, I think it's all about self-preservation and self-promotion with Meadows. If that's what he's about, then good luck to him. It makes no difference to me. But it does piss me off when it affects my job."

"What are you going to do?"

"Do what I normally do. I'll keep my head down, do my job to the best of my ability, and support my team."

"You know you've got the support of the team. As a friend, you've got my unconditional support. Even if you are always taking the piss out of me," Abby said, splashing water from her bottle at Scott.

Beneath all the banter, Scott valued Abby's support and wisdom. Scott didn't have many friends. He'd always preferred to just have a few close friends whom he trusted. Abby fell into that category. Other than Cara, the only other person he could be completely open and honest with was her. And he sensed that in her own inimitable way, Abby felt the same about their friendship.

8

Detective Constable Helen Swift sat patiently in the station's reception area. They'd told her to be there at ten a.m. sharp. She glanced at her phone once again, ten twenty-three a.m. and as yet no one had been by to collect her.

The front desk officer gave her an uncomfortable smile and a shrug.

Helen impatiently tapped the toes of her court shoes on the vinyl floor, the sharp sound echoing off the bare walls. Her stomach flipped over and tightened. She hated first-day nerves. She carried out the same silly habits, habits she wanted to stop, but had yet to achieve it. Her bottom lip was well and truly chewed; she'd checked for the umpteenth time that her blouse buttons were done up to a level resembling decency. She must have stroked her copper-coloured hair and twisted her ponytail around her finger in nervous anticipation a dozen times.

Only one lighter moment relieved her nerves. An elderly man dressed in brown cords and a polyester zipped grey jacket turned up to complain about a group of noisy youths down his road. He was annoyed at how they'd tinker with their cars most evenings and then proceed to roar down the road past his house. The gentleman protested that the youths should have their cars confiscated.

The desk officer looked bored as he leant on the desk and cradled his chin in the palm of his hand. The officer nodded sympathetically while the elderly man tapped his finger on the desk to emphasise the degree of frustration he felt. The stronger he protested, the harder he tapped his finger.

Helen adjusted her light blue suit jacket once more. Part of her still missed the buzz of her old job, as well as the friendships and challenge. But she knew that to follow her own personal desire to progress, she needed a change. Coming to Brighton was a step up in her career progression and an opportunity to work directly on local cases. Doubt flashed in her mind as to whether this move would live up to her expectations.

The buzz on the double doors jogged her back into the present. Detective Superintendent Meadows pushed them open, then held the door open with one foot.

"DC Swift, good to see you again. Please come through," he said, nodding in the direction of the corridor behind him. He adjusted his red tie and offered the slightest of welcoming smiles through tightly pursed lips. There was no mention of an apology for keeping Helen waiting.

"I trust you're all settled in?" he asked as he led her through the corridors up to CID.

"Yes, sir. I'm looking forward to meeting the rest of the team and the fresh challenge. I've rented an apartment in Hove and spent the last few days exploring the area to get my bearings." Helen marched behind Meadows up the stairs.

"Excellent. CID are a good bunch here. Detective Inspector Baker is a strong officer and good at getting the best out of his team," Meadows said, pausing outside a set of swing doors. "Now, as I'm sure you're aware, the team has had a rough ride with the loss of an officer."

Helen nodded. "How are they coping with Officer Mason's loss?"

Meadows crossed his arms and pursed his lips once again, keen to find the right words. "It's been a challenge, but they've been very robust, focused, and professional. Understandably, some have found it harder than others."

Meadows pushed through the doors and strode into the office with Helen in tow. He made his way over to where Scott and the team were gathered around the incident board.

Scott paused for a moment and looked up; the team swivelled in their chairs to see Meadows approaching.

"Scott, you no doubt remember Detective Constable Helen Swift. We have the pleasure of welcoming her to our unit," Meadows announced. He stood to one side and waved Helen through as one might when welcoming royalty.

Helen blushed as warmth spread to her cheeks. Starting a new job was never a comfortable experience for anyone. Having several pairs of eyes on her added to that awkward stand-off moment where she wasn't quite sure whom she should greet first.

Scott stepped forward and extended his hand to welcome her. "DC Swift, good to see you again, and welcome aboard," he said with a warm smile and a strong handshake.

Meadows made his excuses and wished Helen well before leaving Scott to take over.

"Let me introduce you to the members of the team. This is DS Abby Trent, DC Raj Singh, and DC Mike Wilson."

The team all rose and exchanged pleasantries and handshakes.

"Grab yourself a seat, Helen, and DS Trent can show you to your desk later. There's no time like the present to get up to speed with the current case. We're investigating the disappearance of a student from Sussex University by the name of Hailey Bratton," Scott announced, tapping a picture of Hailey on the incident board. "Last seen forty-eight hours ago. Coincidence or not, her boyfriend, Freddie Coltrane, was brought in last night for being drunk and disorderly in town. He was denied access from several bars before becoming verbally abusive and violent towards door staff. He was arrested and slept it off in the cells."

"What's the mood like on campus, guv?" Helen asked.

"The student population are anxious and worried. That's understandable. The staff, the on-site security team, and the local police have done all they can to try to reassure the student population. That's why it's imperative that we get on top of this case as soon as possible."

"What more do we know about Hailey?" Abby asked.

Raj held his pen up in the air. "I've spoken to Hailey's parents. Naturally, they're very upset and concerned. They've cooperated with local police, and having spoken to her parents and the officers, the conclusion is that Hailey's a fun-loving girl. She's never in trouble, she studies hard, and her parents are at a loss to explain her disappearance."

"Mike?"

"Guv, I had a chat with her flatmate, Sophie Smith. She's reiterated similar thoughts to what Raj extracted. Hailey's studying history and politics and really enjoying the course. She's in the debating society and plays on the university netball team. A well-rounded student from all accounts. Sophie can't explain why Hailey's disappeared. She didn't think Hailey was in any trouble, nor did anything seem to be bothering her. She'd always tell Sophie if she was staying out with Freddie, or roughly what time she'd be back. She seems to be quite sensible."

"Okay, cheers, Mike." Scott nodded slowly as he

processed the information. "Did you get hair fibres and her toothbrush?"

"Yes, guv. We've got those in the evidence room. I've also checked in with the CCTV control room on campus. We've drawn a blank there. There's too much of the campus to cover and not enough cameras. It's a big sprawling campus with lots of green space, trees, and paths, which are well lit, but it's a basic set-up. It would be sheer luck to catch her on camera or anything suspicious."

"Anything on her email or social media profiles?" Scott asked.

"We've got her laptop. It is password protected. I've already sent it to the tech team to see if they can access the hard drive for us. We've searched her room. The usual student pit, I'm afraid. More clothes on the floor than hanging up. There were empty alcohol bottles lining the windowsill and posters on the walls. Nothing looked untoward, and Sophie couldn't see anything missing to suggest she'd run away."

Scott nodded his approval. "She's well liked, has a boyfriend, studying well, has no worries or emotional problems that we are aware of, and her disappearance is completely out of character. That doesn't give us much to go on, does it?" Scott mumbled, mostly to himself.

He continued, "And no other students had any suggestions, concerns, or suspicions? She didn't have any run-ins with anyone?"

Silence fell amongst the team, a collective expression of blank faces staring at the incident board. A picture of Hailey Bratton stared back at them, her striking features crystal clear – a picture that had been passed to them by her parents. Her dark brown almond-shaped eyes radiated a warmth and softness that contrasted with her fiery red, long curly hair and pale skin.

"Any news from the phone company?" Scott asked Raj.

"Not yet, guv. I've asked for a triangulation to pinpoint where her phone was last used. I should get the results within the next few hours."

"Don't wait for them, Raj. Get on the blower and push it along. Make sure they understand the urgency of the request."

Raj nodded and furiously scribbled on his notepad.

Scott glanced over to Helen. "Considering this case is completely new to you and with a fresh set of eyes, is there anything we're overlooking?"

Helen furiously scanned all the information and bullet points that were already on the incident board. Friends, social media profiles, last known location, emotional/mental health issues, character.

"The only thing I can think of is trying to pin down her last known movements. Who she was with? If anyone followed her? That type of stuff."

"That's sketchy too, guv," Raj said. "She told Sophie that she was heading into town in the afternoon to get a few bits. Then she was heading up to see Freddie up at the East Slope bar in the evening. Her plan was to stay the night. As we now know, she never got there. CCTV footage on the door shows Freddie coming in and staying for a bit before leaving, but no sign of Hailey arriving at all."

9

The bland interior and bleakness of the interview room created a cold, lifeless atmosphere. A light brown desk with two sets of plastic chairs either side did little to break up the monotony of the room. Light cream walls were split by the emergency panic strip halfway up that ran around the circumference of the room.

As Scott and Abby entered the room, Freddie Coltrane sat hunched in one chair. Scott noticed that Freddie appeared on edge as he wrung his hands and occasionally stopped to pick at the skin on the end of his fingers. He looked decidedly worse following his drunken outbursts last night. He was unshaven and dressed in a crumpled blue shirt and jeans.

The interview with Freddie Coltrane had been delayed whilst the officers waited for Stuart Beecham, the family solicitor, to attend the interview. Freddie's family had been insistent on his right to have legal representation.

Stuart Beecham sat sombre faced alongside Freddie. Beecham's neatly combed brown hair was short and tidy. He had strong angular features and was immaculately turned out in a grey pinstripe suit, crisp white shirt, and dark blue tie. With a pen and paper in hand, he was poised like a coiled rattlesnake, ready to pounce if the officers asked anything that he deemed Freddie had no need or desire to answer.

Scott had done the formalities and introductions, including the caution and Freddie's right to leave whenever he wanted.

"Freddie, we weren't expecting to see you so soon," Scott said. "What concerns me is Hailey is missing, yet you were out last night on a bit of a bender."

Freddie glanced over at Beecham, who gave him the slightest of nods to confirm that it was okay to reply.

Freddie cleared his throat. The stench of stale alcohol wafted across the table in Scott's direction. "I was just letting off steam. It ain't an offence, is it?" He shrugged.

Abby noted Freddie's responses as she closely scrutinised his words.

Scott shook his head. "Of course not, Freddie. It's just a little surprising that your girlfriend's been missing for two days, and if I'm being honest, you don't seem bothered."

Freddie stiffened as he pulled his shoulders back. His jaw tightened as he glared at Scott. "I'd hardly say she was my girlfriend. And as I said to you when you came to see me, she's done a runner with my money. She bled me dry, so I reckon I've got a right to be fucked off." His face relaxed as he stared up at the ceiling. "She's probably moved on to another bloke to leech off."

"And that bothers you?"

Freddie shrugged once again. "Yes, it bothers me. It bothers me that she fleeced me. I was a mug for falling for it."

He pushed up his shirtsleeves before resting his elbows on the table. Scott noticed what appeared to be fresh scratch marks along Freddie's forearms. He and Abby exchanged a knowing look.

"Where did you pick those up?" Scott asked, nodding at Freddie's arms.

Freddie glanced at the red welts and hurriedly pulled his sleeves down to hide them before flicking his gaze between Abby and Scott. "Dunno. Must have happened last night. But I can't remember much of what happened. Maybe it was the bouncers being unnecessarily heavy-handed with me?"

"Did you and Hailey ever fight, and by that, I mean physically?"

Stuart Beecham interrupted before his client could respond. "My client is willingly attending this interview and has cooperated with questions about the events of last night. I fail to see how questions about his relationship with his girlfriend have any bearing on those events," he said sternly.

"I'm just trying to build a better picture of his relationship with Hailey, and why Freddie seems to be so angry about it," Scott said.

"My client is here because he was arrested last night for being intoxicated and the alleged assault of security personnel at a drinking establishment in town. I would kindly ask you to refrain from asking irrelevant questions. Any further deviation in questioning will result in me instructing my client to respond to further questions with no comment. I hope I make myself clear?"

A knock at the door cut through the tension. Mike stuck his head in.

"Guv, a word?"

Scott announced his departure for the recorder before stepping out into the corridor.

"How are you getting on in there, guv?" Mike asked.

"I'm fishing at the moment. His brief is a bit of a stick in the mud. I can't quite make out Coltrane. His girlfriend's been missing for a few days, and he's on the piss in town."

"Well, this may help, guv. We've had the initial feedback

from the tech team about Hailey's laptop. Buried in her folders are quite a few pictures. They look like phone downloads of Hailey in compromising positions with Freddie and another girl. It looks like Hailey and Freddie had a thing for threesomes."

Scott raised his eyebrows in surprise. "I wasn't expecting that."

"Me neither, guv."

"Do we know who the other girl is?"

"Yes, guv. She's got a Facebook and Instagram profile, and they're all connected as friends. Her name is Lucy Wheeler, another student up at the uni. And we've also started to pull off phone records. There are lots of calls between the three of them. It may have been a bit of a regular thing for them."

Scott folded his arms and stared at the floor. He took a few paces back and forth, trying to fit the pieces together.

Was Freddie involved in Hailey's disappearance? Were all three willing participants in this threesome? Might there have been jealousy?

"Okay. Good work, Mike. Anything else?"

"Yes, guv. Triangulation data suggests that Hailey's phone was last used in and around the area of Preston Street. They can't be more precise than that. So give or take a few hundred yards."

"Get onto CCTV control. Check records from forty-eight to seventy-two hours ago in and around the Preston Street and Weston Road area going right down to the seafront."

"I'll get onto it straight away, guv."

Scott paused for a moment before re-entering the room. What he had just discovered painted a different picture of the dynamics in Freddie and Hailey's relationship. As much as he was keen to explore it further with Freddie right now, it made more sense not to divulge it during this interview.

He entered the room and sat down. The recording was resumed.

"Freddie, we will process you in relation to the events of last night in due course. But whilst you're here, we would appreciate your help in trying to build a better picture of Hailey and what she was like. We're concerned for her safety, and I'm sure you appreciate that her parents are extremely worried and wish for her safe return."

Freddie shrugged his shoulders. "I'm sure she'll turn up."

"How would you describe your relationship with Hailey?"

"We've been through this!" he snapped.

"I know we have, but I'm just trying to build a better picture in my mind," Scott said.

"We had a good laugh. We both enjoyed a good drink, and as I said, we'd go back to my place and get down to business."

"Business?" Abby interrupted.

"Sex. S-E-X. Sex." Freddie tapped out each letter on the desk with his finger.

Stuart Beecham interrupted again. "I fail to see how this is relevant to the events of last night."

Freddie raised his hand to silence his solicitor. Confidence was replacing his anxiety. Arrogance was replacing his humility. "It was pretty good. She was a good girl. Not as fruity as I would like, but she was game for having a good time."

"Not as fruity? Can you elaborate?" Scott asked.

Freddie tapped the side of his nose and smiled. "That would be telling, wouldn't it? Let's just say that after a few drinks, she would loosen up. Know what I mean?" Freddie winked at Abby.

"Did you ever force her?" Abby asked.

"As I said, after a few drinks, she was always game."

Scott concluded the interview not long after. The security

personnel at the bar in town had opted not to press charges, leaving Freddie to be processed for being drunk and disorderly with a caution.

Scott's instincts told him that there was more to Freddie than met the eye. What he'd noticed was how very little eye contact Freddie had given during the interview. He was either incredibly shy, or he was hiding something.

It was a point that Abby had picked up as they made their way back to the office. She had noticed Freddie's reluctance to speak until they got onto the subject of sex.

Yes, Freddie is hiding something. The question is what?

10

Upper Lewes Road was one of those streets in Brighton with high-density housing. A busy, narrow road with terraced houses offering little in look or character. Many dwellings had little or no front garden, so residents and passers-by shared the congested space.

Situated within minutes of the University of Brighton main site, Upper Lewes Road and its surrounding side streets housed many student bedsits. The houses had been split and then split again, to house as many students as possible within each property.

Having found the address where Hailey was living, and not seeing a doorbell, Scott loudly knocked on the turquoise door and waited. The tatty door hadn't had a lick of paint in many years. Road grime, discarded crisp packets, and strips of cellophane had found a home in the doorway.

Scott was about to knock again when he heard the latch and chain being released. A small petite woman looked through the gap.

"Yes, can I help you?" she asked in a soft voice. Her bright blue eyes, her pale blemish-free complexion and tightly cut bleached blonde hair made her look deceptively young.

Scott and Abby both produced their warrant cards. "I'm Detective Inspector Baker. This is my colleague Detective Sergeant Trent, from Brighton CID. We're investigating the disappearance of Hailey Bratton. And you are?"

"I'm Sophie Smith, her flatmate," she replied softly. Her impish looks and large doe eyes added to her look of vulnerability.

"We understand that you were the one who reported Hailey missing?" Scott asked.

Sophie nodded as she tucked her hands into her pockets.

"May we come in? We just have a few questions to ask you."

Sophie's face softened further. She stood to one side to let them in. "I'm not sure there's anything else I can say. I've already spoken to the police and answered all their questions. I guess you haven't been able to find her?"

Sophie led them through to the lounge, where they were greeted by a mismatch of well-worn sofas and a heavily scratched teak table in the centre. A large TV hung from the far wall of the lounge. The room was basic and functional, with a mixture of prints randomly pinned around the room. It lacked a theme or style.

"I know you've spoken to one of my colleagues, Detective Constable Mike Wilson. However, Hailey has been missing for forty-eight hours, so her disappearance is being given high priority. According to our notes, the last time you saw Hailey was when she said she was heading into town."

Sophie nodded. "She said she wasn't going to be in town for long. Then she was going to grab the bus up to Sussex uni to spend the evening with Freddie. She gave me one of her cheeky winks and told me not to expect her back until the morning."

"Just before she left, was there anything that gave you the impression that something was bothering her, or that she was upset about anything?" Scott asked.

"No, nothing. She just seemed her normal self. I must admit I didn't like the fact that she was going to see Freddie and spend the night with him. He's such a perv."

Abby and Scott exchanged the briefest of glances.

"Perv?" Scott inquired.

Sophie tucked her elbows in and shrugged. "He's not my type. He thinks he's God's gift to women. The minute Hailey's back is turned, he's chatting to other girls, and he's always up at the East Slope bar. He's such a lech. If you go to the clubs in town, he'll be there. He's just a desperate saddo."

"And Hailey never saw that? It didn't bother her?" Scott continued.

"What's the saying – 'Love is blind' or something? I did try to tell her that he's a bit of a perv. But I didn't want to piss her off or make it sound like I was jealous of that disgusting tosser. She was – is besotted with him. She kept saying that he's her bit of rough. She would go gaga whenever she saw him."

"Was there anything else about Freddie that concerned you?" Abby chipped in.

"Listen, he likes groping girls. He gets off on it. And he's made no secret of the fact that he loves really rough sex." Sophie pulled a pained expression. "Hailey told me that Freddie wanted her to come with him to some BDSM chamber in town where they could both let loose."

Abby offered a nod. "And did she?"

"Not as far as I know..." Sophie trailed off and stared at the floor. "She loves Freddie like mad. She'd do anything for him, so maybe she has. She started smoking weed, and she was never into that before him. She'd even agreed to take part in threesomes just to keep Freddie happy."

"Do you know who Lucy Wheeler is?" Scott asked, studying Sophie's face for any sign of reaction.

Sophie rolled her eyes before looking away. "That's who they invited into bed with them. Her morals – well, let's just say she doesn't have any. Everyone knows she puts it about. A few drinks and she will jump into bed with anyone or anything. Male, female, she's not fussy. I think Freddie finds her exciting. They're both shallow and disgusting people."

Scott cleared his throat at Sophie's comment. "To save time, do you know where we may find Lucy Wheeler?"

Sophie offered a sarcastic laugh. "If she's not in Freddie's bed, then she'll be in her own. Lucy's in the next block from Freddie's room at East Slope."

11

"I know student life can be a bit raucous, but this is taking the piss now!" Abby said as they once again made their way up to the East Slope accommodation. "And there's me thinking that their tuition fees were so they could study."

Scott held the door open for Abby. "Well, that's student life for you. Drinking, sex, experimentation, studying, and learning about independence."

Abby knocked on one of the dorm doors. She was greeted by a loud and strong female, "Coming!"

A tall curvaceous, dark-haired female answered the door. Abby noticed how the girl's pink, thin knitted crop top barely stretched over her chest and past her ribs. Her pierced navel showed off a red stone.

"I'm Detective Inspector Baker, and this is my colleague Detective Sergeant Trent, from Brighton CID. Are you Lucy Wheeler?"

The girl nodded as she straightened her already long straight glossy brown hair that tumbled over her shoulders and partially covered her chest. If she had any fear over two police officers arriving on her doorstep, she was hiding it well.

She waved them through with a large, warm smile. "How can I help?"

"We are investigating the disappearance of Hailey Bratton. We understand you may know her?"

Lucy's dark brown eyes smouldered as a wry smile broke on her face. She shrugged. "Oh, I know her. She's a fun girl."

"And when did you last see her?"

Lucy frowned at Scott and shook her head. "Not sure, probably a few days ago."

"And how did she appear to you at the time?"

"Fine. Normal."

"Would you care to elaborate on how you actually know her?" Scott continued.

"She's going out with my boyfriend, Freddie."

The officers looked at each other.

Scott asked, "And does Freddie have a surname?"

Lucy laughed. "Coltrane."

An uncomfortable pause followed as Abby made some notes.

Lucy added, "Oh, I know what you're thinking, that I'm going out with him and she's going out with him, and I'm not bothered...? Let's just say we have an interesting and open relationship. Neither of us wants to be tied down with one partner. After all, we are still young and like to have fun."

"And how long has this been going on?" Abby pointed her pen at Lucy.

"A few months, six, maybe more. I hooked up with Freddie first. But Freddie being Freddie couldn't keep his hands to himself."

"Has anything happened between the three of you that perhaps could account for Hailey's sudden disappearance?"

Lucy shook her head. "Erm...I don't think so."

"You don't sound so certain," Scott probed. "Hailey's disappearance is causing a lot of heartache for her friends and family. You need to tell us anything that you may know."

Lucy held her hands up. "Hey, listen. I've got no beef with anyone. It's Hailey who has the problem. I think she's been getting a bit too clingy and thinks this *relationship* she has with Freddie is a bigger deal than it is. The fact is Freddie isn't like that. We both really love sex more than anything else." She sighed. "Hailey is a very attractive girl, and we both fancy her. Who wouldn't? She was always very willing to please Freddie. He suggested getting together with me as well. Hailey was a little reluctant to begin with, but with a few drinks inside her, she was game."

Scott's phone beeped. He pulled it from his top pocket and gave the message from Raj a cursory glance. He raised an eyebrow and tutted. Abby glanced at him curiously.

"That's nearly all for now," Scott said. "Just a few last questions. Did you and Freddie ever fight?"

"No. We were either too pissed or off our faces to bother getting angry."

"How about with Hailey – did you fight with her? Or have any disagreements with her?"

"I had no need to. She did phone me a few times a little upset, to tell me how much she loved Freddie, but I didn't really have time for her sob stories."

Scott thanked Lucy, and they left her room.

Scott and Abby strolled back through the campus grounds. The calm open space and shaded greenery offered a stillness and serenity that was in marked contrast to the notions and theories that were rolling around inside Scott's head.

Freddie was a darker character than Scott had initially assumed. Raj's message had been to inform him that Freddie had kicked off in the cells and had needed restraining. His aggression had escalated towards one of the female officers restraining him.

Why did Hailey get mixed up with someone like Freddie, a man who shows very little loyalty or respect towards women?

12

The man reflected on his last acquisition.

"Hailey, Hailey, how sad, how tragic that you had to leave us so early. We were only just getting acquainted, but needs must, and I needed to move on. I hoped you would have stayed a bit longer. We both did, didn't we, Sally?"

The laptop screen was awash with dozens of photos he'd taken of Hailey while stalking her. She'd been unaware of him as he moved in the shadows, blending into the surroundings until the ideal opportunity presented itself to grab her.

He'd tracked her for weeks, monitoring and recording her every move. He'd enjoyed watching her many visits to Charcoal Grill and Perfect Pizza Express on Lewes Road to grab the student special deals. She'd never seen him on the many occasions that he'd sat hunched on the ground. To the average person walking past, he was just another homeless vagrant begging for spare change. He'd dressed in tatty jeans and an old overcoat that he'd bought from a second-hand clothes store in Trafalgar Street, in the heart of the North Lanes.

Her every move had been captured on camera, especially her weekly visits to the nail and beauty bar opposite the Spar. He loved the fact that she took so much pride in her appearance. Her eyebrow appointments, manicures and pedicures just made her even more delectable to him. He hadn't been disappointed when he'd finally captured her. His mind had spun faster than a washing machine spin cycle as he'd carefully undressed her before placing her in the box.

The box was almost ready to receive its next resident.

A thin rubber hose hung through a hole he'd drilled in the lid of the container. It would be connected to an inverted water bottle, allowing water to empty into the mouth of his next captive – if he felt generous, that was. If Sally liked her, that approval would allow him to keep his captive alive for longer.

He liked to learn. He wanted the container to evolve and extend his pleasure. For that reason, he'd drilled a few holes in the metal sides. They'd allow air in, but would also allow him to enjoy the pungent odours of human sweat and bodily fluids that would no doubt escape. He looked forward to taking in the smell of their sweat, piss and shit.

He wanted a new friend to touch, to stroke, to hold. The excitement swirled in his mind and sent shivers through him like a 240-volt lightning bolt racing down his spine. He wanted to watch his next victim squirm away from his hands as he reached out to touch them.

He liked it a lot when they did that. Pain for her, pleasure for him. Captivity for her, a release for him.

He laughed as he remembered Hailey's final moments. Robbed of lucid thought, she had relented and allowed him to worship her body one last time. He couldn't wait to lie down and smell the fresh scent of a new woman, to feel her smooth skin. There would be no one to hear her except him, no one to understand her plight except him.

He knelt down by the container and felt the raw excitement swell within him. His hands shook as he leant forward and stroked the cold metal ready to receive its new guest. Every square centimetre inside and out had been meticulously cleaned twice over with bleach wipes. The faint smell of ammonia lingered and tightened his lungs.

He stood there alone, but the voice inside his head spoke to him again. He nodded as he listened before replying. "I'm glad you like my creation, Sally. After all, you helped me to get here. I did exactly as you asked, and now we'll receive new blood, the nectar of life, and I promise that this one will be even better than Hailey."

"I love you, Sally. I love you with all my heart; no one understands me like you; no one has ever listened to me like you have. You're mine forever."

He climbed in and slowly pulled the lid down over himself. He closed his eyes and inhaled, then drew his legs up to his chest and pulled them tight into his body, like his victim would. Light permeated through the holes that he'd drilled in the walls, offering a tantalising connection with the outside world.

It was the only place left to hide from those who should have loved him.

Their voices filled his head. "We'll show you. You think you can spy on us, you little shit?" And then he was falling, falling down the stairs. Two hands slapped him on the back. Pain radiated through his body. And then the girl was sitting on his back, slapping him. "You pervert." Laughter echoed around him.

He remembered the nice teacher at school who had kept him warm with a blanket whilst they waited for the ambulance to arrive. The weeks in hospital were now nothing more than a shadowy recollection. It had taken many months of rehabilitation to help him walk again. His parents had been told he'd suffered a brain trauma, and that some of his critical thinking might never return. They had spoken about neurochemical imbalances, but he had never really understood what it all meant.

The darkness of the container and the eerie chill jolted him. He could feel the anger surge deep within his belly once again; the rage he felt stiffened every muscle. He forced himself to think of his next captive, smiling as he imagined touching her, smiling as she gave herself to him.

The next opportunity couldn't come quickly enough. He needed to prove to Sally that he loved her and would do anything for her. She had always told him to be more expressive in how he felt, and to find new ways to connect with people.

"If you're happy, then I'm happy," she had told him. Sally always knew what to say to make him feel better.

He reached down and felt the hardness in his groin. It throbbed and twitched, desperate to be touched, desperate to feel skin-on-skin contact once again. He would show them all the closeness he was capable of giving. He wasn't a pervert. He'd loved girls growing up. He loved women; he loved Sally.

He'd show them time and time again. The process needed to start soon – Sally demanded it, and he was keen to please.

13

It was news that no investigating team wanted to hear. The team had been scrambled late in the evening following the reports of a body having been discovered.

Scott's mind buzzed as he approached the scene. The headlights from his car danced in the blackness as he cautiously drove down the single-lane track. Tall shrubbery lined his route, occasionally breaking to expose fields beyond. With his headlights providing the only illumination, the road felt claustrophobic, and darkness closed in from all sides.

He had been preparing a meal for the evening. Cara was due to join him following an extended shift at the mortuary. An evening of good food, wine and amazing company was something Scott had been looking forward to. He'd gone to the effort of preparing his signature dish, piri-piri marinated butterfly chicken and wild rice, to only throw it back in the fridge, disappointed.

Blue flashing lights punctured the darkness ahead of him. The rhythmic pulses of blue light bounced off the surrounding trees and woodland, momentarily shaping the blackened wilderness.

Scott pulled up behind a long line of emergency vehicles. A fire engine, an ambulance, a paramedic car, and several police cars formed an orderly queue on the grass verge ahead of him.

Mike and Helen had been on the late shift when the call had come through. They were the first members of the team on-site. Scott stood by the scene guard just as Abby pulled up behind his car. Scott signed into the scene log and grabbed a packet that contained the usual white paper disposable overalls, gloves, and blue plastic overshoes.

"I was literally just nagging the kids to have their showers and get ready for bed. Any more on what we've got?" asked Abby as she signed in and grabbed a pack.

"I know as much as you. Cara was due to head over to me this evening. She's somewhere over there," he said, nodding about twenty yards ahead where a series of bright arc lights lit up a group of trees.

A section of wired fencing by the side of the road had been cut by the fire service to enable easy access to the wooded copse and the body. They climbed the shallow grassy incline that led farther ahead. Scott's and Abby's torches barely punctured the blanket of darkness.

Scott squinted as they came under the piercing glare of the arc lights that had been set up by SOCO. Matt Allan, the crime scene manager, was overseeing the evidence gathering, whilst Mike and Helen were comparing notes and observing from a distance.

Scott could see the figure of a woman slumped between two trees. The tautness of the ropes securing her wrists had stopped her body from falling forward. Her knees hovered a few inches above the ground. Her head hung forward, and matted red hair obscured her face like an ill-fitting wig.

"Jesus." Scott gasped. "What have you gathered so far, Mike?"

Mike adjusted the mask over his mouth. "Guv, the local farmer discovered her a few hours ago. Well, his dogs did. He's pretty shocked, to be honest. He doesn't visit this part of his land that often but was doing a quick sweep for fly-tippers who've been using his land recently."

"What have we got in the surrounding area other than his farm?"

"Local officers have said there's the Happy Valley riding school on the other side of the road a bit farther up, and that's about it. It's a single-lane track, primarily used for people to access the riding school and for the farmer and his staff."

Happy Valley...hardly. Ironic, Scott thought as he looked around. "Is it Hailey?"

"We can't be certain yet, guv. She's too messed up. But my hunch is it could well be."

Scott nodded in agreement. From his vantage point, she certainly seemed to match the height, weight, and description.

"Helen has already lost her dinner tonight," Mike said as he looked back at the sheepish DC who hid behind her face mask. "You need to go around to the front of the body and have a look."

Scott followed Abby, who had done just that. She stood a short distance back to look at the victim. She winced, and her eyes narrowed when she saw Scott approaching. She shook her head in disgust.

Scott looked at the victim and froze as he caught sight of a huge laceration wound across the front of her abdomen and parts of her intestinal tract hanging down towards her pelvis. His eyes tracked up from her navel to her shoulders. Dark rivers of blood had congealed and dried to form streaky trails that snaked down her body.

"What the hell?!"

Any thoughts of a cosy dinner with Cara were well and truly extinguished as his stomach swirled.

Scott buried his fists deep into his armpits. The positioning of Hailey's body and the way in which she had been bound suggested some form of torture or crucifixion.

Two scenes-of-crime officers covered from head to foot in white made their way around the body. One officer took swabs and samples; the other marked out crucial markers of evidence on the earth before the bright flash of her camera captured the area in detail.

Scott watched Cara go about her meticulous review of the body. She moved gracefully and respectfully around the body as if she wished to avoid rousing the deceased. She took a few steps closer to the body before stepping back to add further notes to her records. She circled the body several times more, paying attention to the smallest of details.

Matt Allan joined Scott and Abby. "Sometimes you think you've seen it all, and then the job throws a curveball like this. I guess you want the initial findings?" he asked, not looking up from his notes that he was writing in partial darkness.

"Well, we're hardly waiting for a bus, are we, mate?" Scott said on a heavy sigh.

"No. I guess not, Mr Grumpy."

Matt's assessment of Scott's mood was accurate, to say the least. On a night off, getting called out to a job was an accepted but unwelcome norm.

Matt said, "Dr Hall can confirm this during the post-mortem, but early indications suggest the victim has been here for more than twelve hours. More likely she's been here nearer to twenty-four. The lacerations and damage to the skin on the lower half of her body looks like it was primarily due to animal activity. There is evidence of puncture wounds, bite marks, and small bits of flesh have been torn off."

"So foxes, rats and other yucky creatures have been getting a free meal?" Abby asked as she visibly shuddered at the thought.

"Yep, pretty much." Matt chewed on the top of his pen, then pointed at the body. "The laceration marks around her shoulders and arms are more likely from birds."

Cara gingerly retraced her steps out of the immediate crime scene to join the others. She pulled her shoulders back and took in a large lungful of air.

"Not a pretty sight unfortunately, Scottie. I can examine her properly when I get her back. Early indications suggest death was more than twelve hours ago. Livor mortis is present in the lower limbs, primarily the thigh and knee section where they're bent back at a near ninety degrees. There's also some discoloration present in the shin region. The primary cause of death was excessive blood loss. You can't see too well from here, but she's got a deep wound to her neck. I'm almost certain her artery has been severed, judging by the blood loss."

"Age?" Scott asked.

"Hard to tell. Late teens to early twenties." Cara pondered. "Again, I can't be certain under this light, but she does look young."

"Hailey?" Scott suggested, and Abby stood beside him.

Abby shrugged. "Possibly."

"Can we glean anything from the way in which she's bound?" Abby asked.

"That's hard to tell at the moment. We'll look at rope fibres once she's down," Matt replied.

Scott said, "Helen, first thing tomorrow, contact the Happy Valley riding school, and see if they noticed anything suspicious in the last twenty-four hours. Find out if they have CCTV covering the front. Is there anyone over there now?"

"Yes, guv. Uniform have already checked," Helen said. "It's locked up at night. The owner lives on-site around the back of the main unit. She didn't hear a thing and was visibly shaken upon hearing the news."

Other than the illumination from the arc lights and blue strobes from the road, the darkness offered few clues. From their location, Scott found it hard to survey the full crime scene in relation to its surroundings. He deduced that whoever had disposed of the victim knew the area well or had spent some time looking for sites where concealment would delay the discovery of their handiwork. SOCO would be there throughout the night and into the next day gathering evidence and recording the scene. The scene would be secured, which would give him and the team the opportunity to review the site in daylight.

Scott stared at the body for some time. Thoughts raced through his mind. He couldn't be certain if it was Hailey, but the victim bore a resemblance.

14

A renewed energy reverberated amongst the team as they gathered around the incident board. At first light, Scott and Abby had met at the location where the body had been discovered. It had given them both an opportunity to review the crime scene in much greater detail, and its proximity in relation to the surrounding landscape and buildings.

One thing that had struck Scott whilst they walked around the scene was the remoteness of the location. The quietness of the night that they had experienced earlier was in marked contrast to the conditions during the day. Despite its remoteness, it was still within a short drive to the A27 Shoreham bypass. The low rumbling din of traffic from the bypass gave a sign of its closeness.

The officers on scene last night had also discovered a farm outbuilding on the other side of the wooded copse. This now extended the crime scene, and forensics officers would begin a daylight search of the whole cordoned-off area. Other than a few wooden stables in the middle of the field opposite, there was little else except the riding school.

Scott said, "Okay, team. I know we're all incredibly tired, but we now have a body on our hands. We need to move on this quickly."

"Do we have an ID on the vic?" Raj asked.

Scott turned towards the incident board and the bright smiling face of Hailey Bratton. "We believe it to be Hailey. That's our priority now. Can we reach out to her parents? We'll need a formal ID. The body was naked. No other personal possessions were found close by, nor does she have any distinguishing marks."

"Any further update on the evidence gathered, or any reports of suspicious activity, guv?" Helen asked, sipping on a piping hot cup of coffee. Swirls of steam pirouetted as she held the mug up to her lips.

"Still nothing. We're going into this investigation blind. My hunch is that whoever took her there knew the area quite well. Hailey was found on a track primarily serving the farm and the riding school."

"So you're probably looking at staff who work at the riding school and the farm, and I guess customers of the riding school?" Helen asked.

Scott was deep in thought and almost didn't hear Helen's suggestion.

He crossed his arms and paced in front of the incident board. "Add to that delivery supplies and couples enjoying a bit of *fun*..." He trailed off as he combed through anyone else who might go down there. "If it had been an opportunist who didn't know the area, then there's a high probability that the body would have simply been dumped by the roadside. There's no CCTV there and no regular traffic, as it's mainly an access road. It stands to reason that a car could quite easily slip down there, dispose of the body, and leave the scene undetected within a few minutes."

Mike shifted in his seat. He crossed his arms and rested

them on the top of his extended belly. "The chances are the killer knew the area quite well or was local to the area. He knew the area well enough to know that they wouldn't be disturbed. With the A27 down the road, it would be easy to do the deed and disappear into the flow of traffic unnoticed."

The suggestion left the team in silence. The chances of finding the vehicle that the killer used amongst hours of CCTV footage would test even the most vigilant of eagle-eyed officers.

"Okay, let's get cracking. We're working on the assumption it's Hailey Bratton. The victim last night bore a similar resemblance in terms of height, weight, hair colour, body shape and facial characteristics to that of Hailey. And without similar disappearances being reported in the last few weeks on our patch, all indications are that this probably is our missing woman."

Despite the gravity of the situation and the loss of life, the team exuded excitement at the opportunity to track down the killer.

It was a strange reversal of feelings that put police officers at odds with the public. In most cases of a body being found, those connected with the victim experienced deep emotional and psychological distress. Police officers, on the other hand, had to maintain a degree of impartiality. Evidence would be gathered, witness statements would be taken, and the hunt for clues would begin in the gladiatorial battle between the police and the killer.

Scott grabbed the whiteboard marker and began writing out bullet point tasks. "Raj, I want you to keep looking into the links between Hailey Bratton and her boyfriend. Anything that might suggest he posed a danger to her."

Raj nodded and flicked through his notes.

"Mike, go back over the phone records, student feedback, and CCTV footage of where she was last seen. Look for anyone who may have been stalking her or she had run-ins with."

Mike nodded in agreement. He interrupted Scott's instructions. "Further enquiries on campus indicated that Freddie is hard-working but has violent tendencies. Especially when he's had a few pints or a bit of the wacky baccy. The lecturers didn't have a bad word to say about him. But some of the guys that he hung around with did say that he was a bit of a peculiar character. Nice as pie when sober, but an aggressive twat when he was drunk."

"Even more reason to look into him," Scott suggested, pointing at Raj.

"I spoke to a few other female students," Abby said, looking at Mike. "I thought maybe it would be less confrontational, and maybe they'd open up more if they were talking to another female. And my hunch paid off."

"More like we didn't want to frighten the female students with Mike growling at them!" Raj teased.

Abby shook her head and rolled her eyes. "Quite a few of them said Freddie was a bit of a charmer. A ladies' man when sober, but a real jerk and pervy when he was off his face. I'm going to be looking at his medical records, because one of the students said that Freddie suffers from bipolar and OCD."

Scott nodded. "Good call."

Abby added, "I reckon he's got major OCD, guv. Many of them commented on how he was obsessive about washing his hands and cleanliness. Apparently, he used to use the end of his sleeves to open doors because he didn't want to touch the handles. He even went as far as cleaning the knives and forks with a serviette in the canteen because he didn't feel they were clean."

"His room smelt of bleach," Scott added. "I noticed his pencils neatly aligned in a row on his desk."

Abby continued as she flicked through her notes, keen as

ever to help the team to build a much clearer picture of Freddie. "He's the son of a wealthy businessman who owns a high-tech company in Ipswich. Apparently, his dad contributes and donates financially towards good causes at the university. So his son's *misdemeanours* are often overlooked."

"That's a nice cosy arrangement," Mike said, snorting. He rolled his eyes.

"For that, Mike, you can do the digging around on his dad," Scott said. "Get the local officers to have a chat with his father. See if we can find out more about Freddie, including any mental health issues. And see if Freddie ever mentioned Hailey to him."

Scott turned in Helen's direction. She sat bolt upright.

"Helen, I want you to check the sex offenders' register. Check any prisoners who have been released in the past five years. See if anyone has a similar MO to their victims. Abby and I are going to be attending the post-mortem this morning. I think it would be a good idea for you to attend as well."

Scott noticed the unease on Helen's face at the suggestion.

"Not been to many?" he asked her.

Helen shrugged. "To be honest, guv, I've only been to a few and not handled them too well. It's the smell of those places. The last PM I attended was on a body in an advanced stage of decomposition. I passed out when they cut through the skull and the putrefied brain poured out."

"Nice," Scott said.

Abby leant over and squeezed Helen's arm. "Don't worry. We'll be there with you. And if I'm honest, I don't really like those places either."

Helen smiled weakly.

15

The morning was racing away as Scott, Abby and Helen arrived at the mortuary. The early morning warmth had been replaced by a heavy heat and a brilliant sunshine that caused them all to squint as they stepped from the car.

They'd waited at the station for what felt like hours whilst Hailey's father was brought to the mortuary for the identification process. He'd sadly confirmed that it was his daughter.

After being buzzed in, they made their way towards the prep room. It was there that they got the first sign that it had been a busy morning at the mortuary as funeral directors came and went. The usual cloying smell mixed with disinfectant and air fresheners had been overtaken by a dense acrid scent.

Abby scrunched up her nose and quickly covered her mouth. "Oh. That reeks," she managed to say as her eyes watered.

Scott looked sympathetically at Helen; she looked decidedly pallid and unwell.

"You okay?" he asked, placing a hand on her shoulder.

Helen clenched her jaw, nodded furiously, and managed a weak smile. A cold sweat broke out on her face.

"It smells like there are a million dead and rotting rats around us. Anyone would think that someone left a baby's nappy out in the sun for three weeks." Scott shook his head. He sniffed and cleared his throat several times, in a desperate attempt to shake off the stench that clung to the insides of his nostrils and throat. "The sooner we get this over with, the sooner we can leave and get some lunch."

Abby stopped and stared at Scott in bewilderment, her mouth wide open. "Are you for real? What is it with post-mortems and food for you? Every time we come out to one, you always bring up the subject. I then have to sit there and watch you stuff your face afterwards."

Scott smiled and shrugged unapologetically. "What can I say? I love my food."

"Screw and loose come to mind, personally," Abby replied, pushing through the doors.

"Ah, welcome to the party, you three. I thought you'd never get here," Cara said as she glanced up momentarily, her hands buried deep inside the abdomen of the cadaver.

"Dr Hall, this is DC Helen Swift, the newest member of our team," Scott said. "We didn't really get a proper opportunity to introduce you to her last night. Helen, this is Dr Cara Hall, our pathologist."

Cara nodded enthusiastically at Helen. "No need to be so formal; call me Cara. Are you okay with me calling you Helen?"

With her hands tightly wrapped around her chest, Helen said that was fine. Her eyes flicked between Cara and the cadaver.

"Have you been cooking again, Cara?" Scott teased as he waved his hand several times in front of his nose.

"Flattery won't get you anywhere...And I'd be careful if I

were you. You're heavily outnumbered, three to one, so I don't rate your chances." Cara's eyes sparkled wickedly as she glanced at Abby and Helen.

"Sorry about the smell," Cara added. "We had a heavy job in this morning. A middle-aged man died in suspicious circumstances. Somewhere out towards Eastbourne, if I recollect. Unfortunately, they couldn't fit him in quick enough for a PM, so they asked us to help out."

"Bad one, huh?" Scott asked.

"You could say that. To be honest, Neil and I both found it a challenge." Cara glanced at Neil, who scrunched up his eyes and pushed his thick-rimmed glasses back up his nose. "The poor fella had been dead for more than three weeks. He had the whole shebang – flying insects, larvae, maggots and was leaking from places that he shouldn't have been leaking from."

"Poor bugger, they had to scoop him off the sofa...He'd seeped into it." Scott sighed, deciding that Cara had given them too much detail, and moved on. "What can you tell us about Hailey Bratton?"

Hailey's body was laid out on the mortuary table like a museum exhibit. The work of the mortuary team was already at an advanced stage. Her chest and abdomen cavity had been opened up in the traditional Y pattern. Using Cara's preferred method of investigation, the Rokitansky technique, all of her internal organs had been removed in one whole process to be measured and weighed.

Random small flesh bites peppered her body, fully visible in the daylight. Scott concentrated hard on her face, which now clearly matched Hailey Bratton's photo. With her hair neatly combed off her face, her tight, youthful blemish-free skin still offered a delicate attractiveness. Her once red, fiery hair now lay limp and dull.

Cara said, "Okay, let me take you through what I've found

so far. The cause of death is blood loss. The carotid artery was severed, so she would have died within a matter of minutes." She moved farther down towards the cadaver's feet. She lifted and twisted one foot to show the heel. "There are strong abrasions on both heels, and traces of what appears to be a thick black oily substance."

"Ideas?" Scott enquired.

"It's hard to say, some type of thick residue. I've taken a scraping and will send it off for analysis."

Abby jotted details down in her notepad. "Do you know what caused the abrasions?"

Cara tilted her head. "My guess is that she was probably dragged along the ground. There's fresh bruising under her armpits and around the top of her chest. That would suggest that someone had grabbed her under the arms to move or drag her."

Abby nodded at the suggestion.

Cara continued, "There's an indication of some type of sexual assault. There are scratches on the insides of her thighs close to her vagina, and some internal abrasions in line with forced penetration of some sort. There are no distinctive tears, so I wouldn't imagine that any type of instrument was used. We've taken swabs for any DNA. I've also taken scrapings from under her fingernails and toenails."

Scott noticed that certain parts of the cadaver's skin had red irritation and tiny blistering. He pointed at them, hoping to catch Cara's attention.

She spotted him. "I'm not sure about those. They cover large sections of her body. Neil, if you could?"

Together, Cara and Neil rolled the cadaver onto her side so the three officers could examine her back. "As you can see, there's a rash on the back of her arms, her back, shoulders, buttocks and her calves in particular. Again, I've taken skin scrapings, so hopefully that will throw up a clearer idea of what caused them."

The post-mortem continued for some time as Cara went through her investigations. Scott and the team left when Cara was unable to identify any further trauma or injury worth noting.

16

Scott, Abby, and Helen grabbed a corner table in the Munch coffee shop not far from the police station. Abby and Helen sat stony-faced, shaking their heads in disbelief as Scott heartily tucked into a melted ham and cheese panini.

They had valiantly fought hard to keep the contents of their stomachs down during the post-mortem. But now they found themselves once again looking away as stringy bits of cheese hung from Scott's panini and clung to his chin. Helen had passed on ordering anything other than a strong cup of black coffee, which was proving hard to keep down on her already unsettled stomach.

Scott wiped away crumbs from around his mouth and then proceeded to wash everything down with a large, loud gulp of his tea.

"Do you have to be so noisy when you eat?" Abby protested.

"You always have something to whinge about. I just offered to buy you a full fry up, or an egg and sausage sandwich. In fact, anything on the menu, but you moaned it would make you fat!" Scott teased.

Abby gave him one of her sarcastic smiles.

She turned to Helen and said, "Sorry that was a bit of a tough PM. I'd like to say that they get easier, but they don't. It doesn't matter how many PMs you go to, the sights and smells seriously spoil your day, but they are a necessary must. And it's often made worse by the fact that we end up going to eat afterwards. *Don't we, guv!*"

Scott ignored Abby's dig and chose instead to settle up at the counter.

"So what made you choose Brighton?" Abby asked.

Helen shrugged. "I'd been with Cambridgeshire for quite a while, and I just needed a fresh challenge. It made sense to move to a new area, and I love being by the sea too. Here I can push myself a bit with new methods of policing, a new patch and hopefully a different set of problems. Naïvely, I thought it might be a bit quieter here," Helen said with a wink.

"Erm, I think you'll find that it's anything but quiet down here. We cover a big patch. We've got over two hundred entry points along the coast, so drug and human trafficking is quite a big one for us."

Helen nodded slowly.

"What was it like over in Cambridgeshire?" Abby asked.

"It was a big enough set-up. We were part of MCU, the major crime unit, which brought together CID from Beds, Cambridgeshire and Herts. There were about one hundred and seventy of us across the three counties working on serious crimes. It was a real eye-opener, as we had a big patch too and had to work with colleagues from different regions. We basically had two teams headed up by DCIs. One was based at Cambridgeshire HQ in Huntingdon and the other at Hertfordshire HQ in Welwyn Garden City."

"Yes, that does sound impressive. Good for you. Well,

we're looking forward to your contribution to the team. It's a close-knit one, and there's lots of banter between us. And to be honest, you can't get a better guv than the one we've got. But don't tell him that I told you so. His head is already too big." Abby smiled, glancing at Scott.

"Thanks, skip. It's been a bit of a whirlwind the last few weeks, and I've certainly had to hit the ground running, but I'm looking forward to the challenge."

17

Scott felt satiated as he sat back in his office chair. His stomach groaned from the large lunch he'd just eaten. He was regretting having had the portion of fries to go with his panini. That was always his Achilles' heel. His eyes were bigger than his belly.

He began to flick through the dozens of emails that sat unopened in his inbox. Memos, circulars, police federation updates, annual leave requests, together with email updates from forensics and the HOLMES team, which left his inbox creaking at the seams. If there was one thing he hated about his job, it was the admin and endless round of meetings. The sad fact was the higher he progressed up the promotional ladder, the more it took him away from what he loved most – and that was serving the public.

The boredom of flicking through emails was thankfully interrupted by Mike's heavy-fisted knock on his open door.

"Have you got a minute, guv?"

Scott flicked his head to invite him in. "What's up?"

"We had a call come through earlier from an ex-girlfriend of Freddie Coltrane. She's been aware of the increased police presence on campus, which included us making our enquiries on East Slope. She said she'd been meaning to call us for a few days but was just too frightened."

"Go on."

"Her name's Yana Melnik, from the Ukraine. Her story seems to tally with the general consensus about Freddie. She said she was scared of him. One minute he was nice, then nasty when drunk." Mike scanned his notes before continuing, "Yana said his sex games were violent, degrading, and they terrified her."

Scott made his own notes as he jotted down the keywords: *violent, degrading, sex games.*

"That's just for starters, guv. He wanted to mark her with a knife. She sounded shaky on the phone. Yana started rambling on about how he wanted to experience kinky pain."

Freddie's background worried Scott. It wasn't unusual for couples in certain circles to experience a certain type of sexual and physical humiliation. In fact, there was a whole underground scene dedicated to such proclivities. But such activities were always conducted between two consenting adults. Freddie's activities, on the other hand, piqued Scott's interest. It was becoming clear that Coltrane's sexual perversions weren't a welcome addition to the relationships he'd had.

"Okay, good work, Mike. I would normally say that you and Abby go to interview Yana, but I think on this occasion she may feel more at ease talking to two female officers. I'll get Abby and Helen to interview her –"

Scott was interrupted by Meadows striding into Scott's office.

Mike looked between Meadows and Scott, hurriedly made his excuses and left.

"Sir?" Scott asked.

Meadows closed the door behind him and took a seat

opposite Scott. He straightened his tie, crossed his legs and then focused on picking off imaginary flecks of dust from his trousers.

"This ongoing investigation is crucial for our team and the station. There's a lot riding on this case, especially after recent events..." Meadows allowed that thought to hang in the air, likely to reiterate the scrutiny Scott was under. "We think it would be a good idea to put DC Swift undercover on campus."

"I don't think it's necessary at the moment, sir. The investigation has only just begun, and we're still going through all our initial lines of enquiry."

"I appreciate that, Scott, but it's been agreed with the vice chancellor and the vice chancellor executive group at the university. We feel that it would be beneficial for our investigation to have a set of eyes in amongst it all."

"With all due respect, sir, I think I should have been consulted about this before agreement. DC Swift is the newest member of my team. She's still inexperienced. Putting someone undercover is not a decision we should take lightly. Undercover ops should only be used as a last resort."

Meadows was undeterred. "That may be so, Scott, but you're missing the point. We've got a large campus population. We now have a murdered female student and need to avoid any mass hysteria. Clearly, the university is concerned about their reputation. The last thing they want is female students being put off from applying because they fear for their safety. Think about it, Scott. Swift is ideal. She's new to the area, so that allows her to act naïve. She is young and attractive. In my opinion, she would fit in well as a mature student, and Helen would have a better chance of identifying intelligence faster than anyone else on the team."

Scott was treading the fine line between insubordination and following instructions. Sending Helen in was a bad idea.

He shook his head in disagreement, deciding to stick with his gut instinct. The eyes of the force were clearly on him. Whether he wished to be part of their games didn't matter. Meadows was clearly playing cat and mouse with him.

Meadows stood slowly and straightened. He stuffed his hands in his pockets and tilted his head to one side. "She goes in tomorrow, Scott. Brief her; get her ready. No doubt she will jump at the chance. And I'm more than happy to have a chat with her myself. I could tell her about what an excellent opportunity this will be for her."

Scott thought fast. "Sir, I think I have a better and more sensi– I mean, reasonable approach. Instead of putting Helen in undercover, why not put her there in a more visible and reassuring role? We can set her up within the student union for a few days, and female students can go and seek reassurance directly. Helen will also be kept up to date with any concerns or intel on campus."

Meadows paused at the door. He turned to look at Scott. His expression gave little away, but Scott knew he'd given Detective Superintendent Meadows another option, one he hadn't considered.

"I'm not going to risk looking like an idiot in front of the university chancellor, Scott. The plan has been agreed."

Scott smiled. "You won't, sir. Offering a police presence on campus to reassure the population, and one female students would welcome, would be a positive step. With nearly twenty thousand undergrad students, what good would an undercover officer do? It would make far more sense to make DC Swift more visible."

Meadows loitered for a few moments before conceding and agreeing that it would make more sense.

Scott watched as Meadows sauntered out of his office. He glared at the man's back; frustration simmered deep inside him. He hated being anyone's puppet, but Meadows had a knack of gnawing deep into Scott's psyche and winding him up.

Scott left his office and walked over to the incident board.

"Okay, ladies and gentlemen, gather around." He looked from one face to the other. His team looked back with a mixture of inquisitiveness and impatience.

"First things first. Mike, can you arrange a formal search of Freddie Coltrane's room on campus for tomorrow morning? I want that place torn apart. Secondly, Detective Superintendent Meadows has been in discussions with the vice chancellor of the university. It was felt that to speed up the investigation and help us to gather intelligence quicker, it would make sense for an officer to go undercover on campus."

The team exchanged glances of confusion.

Sensing the bewilderment, Scott held up his hands and elaborated, "I know, I know. You're probably wondering why. But we're not here to challenge decisions made by senior officers. I thought best that rather than have a covert presence, we have a visible presence on campus for a day or two to reassure the female population and perhaps pick up any additional information that may assist our investigation." Scott glanced at DC Swift prior to continuing, "It was felt that Helen would be best placed to go on campus, and I'll get a PCSO to help too. Let's be frank, you probably have the best chance of mingling and blending in than us old folk!"

Helen's eyes widened in surprise. The news took everyone by surprise.

Scott pulled up a chair and sat opposite his team. "Helen, how do you feel about this? I know this probably isn't what you expected, and you've been thrown in at the deep end from day one. Listen, I'd fully understand if you have reservations and concerns. And if you're really worried about them, then we can go and speak to the governor and come up with a different plan."

"I have to admit, guv, it wasn't something I was expecting in my first week in a new post, but yeah, that's fine with me," she replied.

"Great, you'll be in there from tomorrow."

18

Edinburgh Road was off the Lewes Road. A typical, nondescript narrow street close to the University of Brighton main campus. The road, together with its neighbouring streets, was the heart of private student accommodation. Endless rows of terraced, dirty white or cream drab houses with little to no frontage dominated the pavement. It was a congested street at the best of times. With cars double-parked either side, it made driving unbearable during peak travelling times. The council had turned the street into a one-way road to ease the flow of traffic.

The man stood outside one door. After knocking a few times to make sure no one was home, he leant into the door to test how securely it had been fastened. The door moved and rattled in its frame, so he leant in harder. This was going to be easier than he had expected.

He checked once again that the coast was clear, and then took one step back and shoulder-charged the door. The simple Yale latch offered little resistance as it surrendered to his weight. The brittle door frame crumbled, and he pushed through into the hallway.

The well-worn beech laminate floor was scuffed and marked through years of neglect as each year new groups of students passed through. A discarded pile of assorted shoes, boots and trainers lay behind the door. A coat rail appeared to hold up far more coats and jackets than it was designed for.

He casually glanced into the communal lounge and noticed the cereal bowls that hadn't been cleaned up after the morning rush. Empty cans of Red Bull, Fanta and Coke were on the table and by the sofa. He shook his head in disgust at the level of untidiness. His sharp sense of smell was working overtime, much to his frustration. A cloying, stale stench hung in the air and assaulted his nostrils. These students clearly didn't understand the concept of ventilation.

The prospect of the rest of the house being cleaner was soon squashed as he picked his way through to the kitchen and the bathroom beyond. In these small, terraced houses, the bathroom was often found behind the kitchen. In student accommodation, one of the bedrooms upstairs was usually squeezed in size to fit in an additional room with a shower and toilet.

He turned up his nose at the squalor in the kitchen. Food crumbs were scattered across the kitchen work surface. Packets of cheap cornflakes and Rice Krispies sat where the occupants had left them. He rolled his eyes when he saw the pile of tea-stained mugs in the sink, waiting for one of the students to volunteer for cleaning duties.

The upstairs didn't fare much better as he moved from bedroom to bedroom. Discarded clothes sat in random piles on the floor. Textbooks and notepads lay on tables as if they had just been emptied out of rucksacks. Curtains hadn't been opened in any of the rooms to let the brilliant summer sunshine in.

"Disgusting, filthy animals," he muttered.

He stuffed hands in his pockets, desperate to avoid picking up any contamination.

Who knows when this place was last cleaned? I should have brought my bleach cleaning wipes or at least a pair of rubber gloves.

He looked into one room, but that wasn't the bedroom he needed. It clearly belonged to a male.

He moved through the upper floor until he found the right one. He was certain that this was *her* room. Passport-sized photographs of her with another friend were pinned above her desk. As he looked through each shot, he noticed they were taking it in turn to pull silly faces. He glanced at a framed picture of her cuddling her dog called Sophie from back home.

How cute, two bitches in the same photograph.

He pulled the drawers one at a time and rifled through the contents. The top drawer held a mixture of Superdry and New Look T-shirts that seemed to be a favourite essential of her wardrobe. The second drawer was the one that excited him the most. An assortment of functional and skimpy underwear dropped in an untidy pile. It stirred feelings within him; it sent his mind into an uncontrollable spin as shivers raced through his body. In the midst of summer heat, fine hairs on his arms stood up as he experienced sensory overload.

Everything he felt for her intensified tenfold as he pulled out one delicate lacy number and studied the intricacy of the lace patterning.

He pictured her wearing them, and how the delicate triangular piece of fabric would hide her most intimate spot from him.

Not for long, my darling.

"You're a fine woman beneath those tatty jeans and skinny tops that you wear. You hide your beauty so well. But I know how much you like to take care of yourself. What a treat you are for any man fortunate enough to worship your body. You are indeed a thing of beauty. It's a shame so many don't like your type. But it just means that you've been saving yourself for me and what I'm about to experience with you."

He placed her underwear back in the drawer. He didn't need to take any souvenirs when he'd be getting her as his main prize. A hairbrush offered everything he was looking for. He pulled a handful of red hair from the bristles and held the twisted mess delicately in the palm of one hand.

With the ball of hair neatly tucked into a small plastic bag, he poked his head out into the street to make sure the coast was clear. The door closed easily and quietly within its broken frame, and he slowly walked away.

He leant up against the wall of a house at the top of the road and flipped open his newspaper. Now all he had to do was wait.

His patience was rewarded less than thirty minutes later when he saw her loom into view. He held his paper up high, catching a look over the top to watch her turn into the road. She was oblivious to the people and environment around her, like most people her age. She was wrapped up in her own world. Distinctive white earplugs were nestled in each ear. She was listening to a song with dreadful lyrics.

He tutted to himself as she passed. How anyone could listen to that garbage, he would never understand.

They've never played that on Smooth Radio.

The hairs on the back of his neck prickled with excitement as he watched her pause by her front door. He watched as confusion robbed her of her faculties, and she glanced up and down the road. An indecisive mixture of curiosity and fear made her take one step forward before taking another step back.

Using one hand, she gently pushed open the door. With

her other, she pulled her earplugs out. He could see her mouth moving but couldn't hear what she was saying. He guessed that she was probably shouting to see if anyone was inside. A warm, smug feeling spread through him as he watched her bravery.

Good girl, in you go.

He watched her take a few cautious steps in through the front door. With her safely out of view, he folded the newspaper, tucked it under one arm and walked away slowly along the Lewes Road, next to the evening rush hour.

She would now know that the house had been broken into. He'd be long gone before the police arrived.

19

The pot of water bubbled on the stove in Cara's kitchen. Steam twisted and pirouetted up from the boiling pan, dancing to its own tune.

Scott had been tasked with chopping the carrots. They had both agreed that they deserved a night in with home-cooked food and a bottle of red wine. Cara was chatting away, telling Scott about new regulations for pathologists.

Scott, only half listening, had paused midway through slicing one. His knife was hovering just an inch or two above the vegetable.

She stopped speaking and looked at Scott. "Penny for your thoughts..." she said.

He gave no response.

"Earth calling Scott. Earth calling Scott..."

Cara still didn't get a response.

It was on her third time of calling, and only when she poked him in his ribs, that Scott jolted back to the present.

"Sorry. I was away with the fairies. What were you saying?" he asked.

Cara tutted and replied, “I was just saying how I wanted to put dark purple streaks in my hair.”

“Really?”

Cara burst out laughing. “No, you doughnut. As if. Anyway, what’s up with you?”

“Oh, nothing important, just work stuff.”

“Well, it must be important if it’s enough to take you away from chopping carrots,” Cara said with a smirk, eyeing the half-chopped carrot.

He sighed. “I’m just not happy about the decision Meadows had initially taken to put Helen undercover. What was he thinking? But to not involve me in those decisions....” Scott jabbed the carrot.

“You’re struggling a bit with all of this, aren’t you?” Cara asked as she came in by his side. She wrapped her arms around him and laid her head on his shoulder.

Scott nodded.

“Do you think he’s got it in for you?”

“I wouldn’t say that. We just don’t see eye to eye. He’s very much into showing officers, especially the senior ones, that he’s in control and that he gets results. Losing Sian was a major blow for all of us. But for Meadows, he took that personally. It’s a blot on his career, and he doesn’t like that. He likes everything clean, tidy, organised and efficient. I think he feels I’m to blame for that blot on his record, and that’s why he gives me a hard time. He’s a cunning bloke.”

Cara furrowed her brow. “What do you mean?”

“Well, he’s into promoting himself as an important and busy officer, someone who has his pulse on everyday policing and the management of his team. I’ve noticed that he only goes to meetings where there’s something of value to him. Other times, for the meeting he doesn’t want to attend, he’ll send apologies for his absence. He’s quick to step in if there’s anything that threatens to rock his ship.”

"And losing Sian rocked his ship?"

"Possibly. Recruiting Helen, then deciding to put her undercover is his way of showing the brass that he's got things under control."

Cara nodded. "It still sounds like he's got it in for you. Bloody politics!" she fumed.

"I think he's just trying to unsettle me," Scott said, anger lacing his tone. "He's probably hoping I'll slip up or challenge him, and in return, it will give him the ammo to have me disciplined or kicked off the force." His tone softened. "But I got him to change his mind, so that's something."

"You know what we need? A break. How about we go away after this case? Just you and me, no work, no distractions, just R & R?"

Scott shrugged his shoulders. The way he felt at the moment, he was struggling to find anything that piqued his interest. The chances of him being able to switch off ranked poorly. Having just lost Sian left him feeling uncomfortable with the idea of being away from them. He dreaded the thought of them thinking he'd gone off on a jolly whilst they were still grieving and coming to terms with the loss.

"I will make it worth your while," Cara whispered in his ear as she softly held his earlobe between her lips. "I'll make sure that you switch off, especially if I'm standing naked in front of you. It's something about being on holiday that makes me feel horny. It must be the sun, sea, and sand that brings out the devil in me."

Cara always found a way to bring a smile to his face. "Are you telling me that you're even *worse* when on holiday? Is that possible?" he teased.

"You've seen nothing yet."

He laughed. "Now you're scaring me."

Cara squeezed herself between Scott and the kitchen work surface. "I'm being serious, Scott Baker. We could do with getting away after the past few months we've had. I think you and I need some *us* time. It would be good for us to get away. We can relax, talk, and maybe even think about our future."

"Now you're really terrifying me," he said with eyes wide in mock fear. "If you're looking for me to make an honest woman of you, dream on."

"Oi, you can go off people really quickly, you know," she said, playfully punching him in the chest. "Scott, you know I love you, and I'd do anything for you. I haven't been this happy in a long time. When I meant talking about the future, I just thought maybe we could look forward to moving in together on a more permanent basis. Wink, wink, and maybe even the patter of tiny feet if you thought the time was right one day?" Cara's voice dropped to a soft murmur.

Scott nodded silently. Hearing those words took him by surprise. There was a part of him that craved stability and a family life. He wanted the chance to feel normal once again. It had been so long that he'd forgotten what normal really meant.

As he stared into Cara's eyes, her warmth reached out and connected with him on a deeper level. He felt comforted and reassured that this woman wanted to be a permanent part of his life.

Cara added, "Now, I suggest you finish preparing the carrots, or I'll stick them where the sun doesn't shine."

"Now, now, there's websites for that type of thing!" he offered with a smile.

20

Freddie Coltrane's door rattled in its frame; the sound echoed up and down the corridor. At this time of morning, most of the students would be fast asleep, and it was for that reason Scott had decided to execute the search now. It gave little opportunity for Freddie to hide anything that might be deemed as incriminating, and it also gave the team the element of surprise.

Scott knocked on the door again.

The way a search was executed depended on each case. If there was a threat to life, or if the suspect was deemed dangerous, or could potentially dispose of evidence such as drugs, then the method of entry tended to be swift, loud and explosive. In such instances, Scott and the team would rely on the tactical entry team, who would use the big red enforcer, a sixteen-kilogramme steel battering ram that officers used to gain entry into properties. However, this method of entry sometimes attracted unwanted and hostile attention, which on occasion led to extra resources being drafted in to protect officers undertaking the search.

On this occasion, it had been agreed with the vice chancellor of the university that a low-key approach was preferred, to avoid unnecessary distress to fellow students. The vice chancellor had expressed his concerns to Meadows as to the necessity of such a search in the first place. With Freddie Coltrane's father being a significant donor to the university, the VC was at pains to suggest that Freddie's father should be consulted first. But Meadows had insisted that Freddie was an adult, and that his father's involvement with university donations wasn't a valid reason to interfere with their investigations.

Scott, not wishing to announce their identity and risk other students hearing, knocked gently again and tried the door handle. The door opened. Scott and Abby exchanged curious glances. He pushed the door open and peered inside.

The room was just as clean and tidy as it had been on their last visit. The curtains were wide open, flooding the room with daylight, and the bed hadn't been slept in.

The element of surprise hadn't turned out the way they'd expected. Freddie Coltrane had clearly left earlier or had not been back all night.

Scott, Abby, and Mike squeezed into the cramped room. The two uniformed officers remained outside.

"Bugger." Scott fumed. He'd been hoping to catch Freddie there. "Where is the little scrote?"

"Your guess is as good as mine, guv," Mike responded. "He could be in any one of these rooms on campus, or he could have crashed on someone's floor in town, or..."

Scott considered the final option. He could have something to hide and was on the run.

He instructed one of the officers to contact local officers in Ipswich via the control room. He needed to make sure that Freddie hadn't done a runner and gone home.

Scott, Abby, and Mike put on blue rubber gloves and placed the empty evidence bags to one side as they split up.

However, in this case, the term split up was really lost in this situation. With the room barely ten feet long and seven feet wide, there was little space to manoeuvre.

Freddie's room was immaculately clean with several packets of bleach wipes and Febreze air freshener sprays sitting on one corner of his desk. The search lasted less than an hour. With just a bed, desk, bedside table, and wardrobe, there was very little searching to be done.

Mike discovered a shoebox at the bottom of Freddie's wardrobe containing incriminating evidence of Freddie's sexual preferences.

Within the shoebox were several items: female underwear, photos, and DVDs, together with a digital camera.

Upon examination of the digital camera, Mike found pictures of naked women performing oral sex on an unidentified white male. Other more disturbing footage was uncovered in videos where a male was performing a forceful act on a female. The woman was clearly in pain and was objecting as she attempted to push his hand away. There were several videos showing similar acts on other women despite their objections.

Further evidence uncovered during the search made Freddie's position of innocence more untenable. A small four-inch-bladed knife was discovered under his bed.

All the evidence was gathered and individually sealed in evidence bags and clearly documented, including a mobile phone.

21

A clearer picture began to form about the lengths Freddie Coltrane would go to satisfy his sexual needs. However, current lines of enquiry uncovered nothing of substance so far to suggest that Freddie was complicit in the death of Hailey Bratton. The questions on everyone's lips were did Freddie have a colourful, extreme, and often aggressive tendency towards sex, but was he capable and willing to commit murder to satisfy that tendency? And where was he?

The team listened intently as they gathered around the incident board. Scott was relaying information on Helen's new assignment on campus, the post-mortem, and forensic reports on Hailey Bratton.

Scott scanned the faces of his team. Many nibbled biscuits that Raj had brought with him to the briefing. Though Scott wouldn't admit it, Raj's continuous supply of snack and treats seemed to provide a lift to the spirits of the team when they most needed it. In a strange way, it gelled the team together.

Food always has a knack of doing that.

"Bollocks," Mike cursed as his Rich Tea biscuit plopped into his tea, the splash back staining his shirt. "They really are a pathetic excuse for a biscuit, right?"

The others laughed at his misfortune.

"You got greedy!" Raj commented as he demonstrated his quick in and out approach to the perfect dunk.

Mike pulled a face as if to imply 'clever clogs'.

"Right, let's crack on," Scott interjected. "I'm sure the dunking debate will continue until the end of civilisation. Helen is in place on campus now, and we've roped in a PCSO to assist her. We've set her up in the student union close to the entrance so anyone can spot her. She is to offer support and advice to female students and hopefully provide some sort of visible reassurance."

The team nodded collectively.

Scott continued, "Post-mortem results concluded that Hailey Bratton did die from extreme blood loss because of a severed carotid artery. There were traces of alcohol and cannabis in her blood. Dr Hall identified several partial human bite marks in and around her neck, breast, and pubic regions. Dr Hall called in a forensic odontologist to examine them immediately, to aid the collection of as much evidence as possible before the characteristics like the shape and size of the marks changed."

He paused so the team members who were taking handwritten notes caught up.

He continued, "However, due to the time that's elapsed between the approximate time of death and the discovery of her body, there was what the odontologist referred to as distortion, which led to the bruising being diffused into the surrounding soft tissues. There were also drag marks, which made the impressions less clear. Nevertheless, photographs and sizing were carried out, as well as swabs for any DNA." Scott passed around the photographs of the bite marks. "We may or may not be able to use dental impressions of any suspects, including Freddie."

The team pored over the photographic evidence, taking a few moments to turn the images through a three-hundred-sixty-degree rotation to get a clearer perspective.

"There were traces of earth and grass found on Hailey's body that match the location where her body was found," Scott said. "The likely cause of the abrasions on her heels is from being dragged backwards. Analysis of the abrasions identified two substances. There was soil matter, which originated from the location in which she was found, and the oily residue, which underwent detailed forensic examination, now identified as marine engine oil. Matt and his team are looking into this further because it would suggest that she may have been kept somewhere where this marine oil was stored."

"Could she have been kept on a boat or a yacht or something like that?" suggested Raj. "After all, we've got many points of entry along the coast where shipping vessels, yachts, or sailing boats can tie up."

Scott nodded, agreeing it was a possibility that couldn't be ruled out. He assured the team that forensics was carrying out further investigations and analyses on the oil to identify its grade, viscosity, and likely use.

"The killer is doing their hardest to cover up their tracks," Scott said. "The red skin scrapings taken from Hailey's body contained traces of ammonia. So that would suggest to me that the body was cleaned with an ammonia-based substance to remove any incriminating evidence such as DNA residue. The highest concentrations of ammonia were found on her arms, back, buttocks, pubic region, backs of legs and palms."

"So it's unlikely we will get any saliva or semen DNA?" Raj asked.

Scott shook his head. "There was certainly nothing found

in the random swabs taken from the skin surface of the body, including the bite marks. However, DNA was found inside her. Nothing has matched on the database yet, but they are now running a comparison with swab samples taken from Freddie."

"What more have we got on Freddie?" Scott asked the team.

Mike flicked through his notes. "I've examined the phone records and CCTV in relation to Freddie's movements. I've also tied his movements to local enquiries. He seems to be a frequent visitor to an S & M place called" – Mike raised an eyebrow – "*Brighton Dungeon*. I suggest we pay them a visit."

Abby rolled her eyes and said, "Yes, I bet you'll be first to volunteer."

Scott ignored the ribbing. "Mike, keep digging. See if you can find any CCTV footage of vehicles in and around the location of where Hailey's body was found. Then cross-reference against the riding school and the farm, and let's see if that throws up anything."

Abby said, "Guv, Raj and I went and had a chat with Freddie's ex-girlfriend Yana Melnik. She's confirmed what we already know about Freddie. She said he was sadistic and perverted. He wanted to do things to her that she wasn't comfortable with. She agreed to some acts; others she didn't. She asked him to stop on many occasions, but he continued to commit sexual acts on her. She said that he turned aggressive with her on more than one occasion and pinned her to the bed by her throat when she rejected his advances." She pursed her lips in frustration.

From the reports coming in, it was becoming clear that Freddie Coltrane was a serial sexual deviant and predator. Scott's assumptions were reinforced when Abby said that Yana mentioned how Freddie's eyes would light up when he talked about bodies being mutilated.

"Okay, thanks, Abby. We need to pull out all the stops now to either confirm or eliminate Freddie from our enquiries. Raj, I want you to pull up everything you can find on Freddie. Go back as far as his school. Then pull up all his medical records, dental records, bank statements, etcetera. If he's implicated in any way with Hailey's death, then we need those answers now. And then we need to find him."

22

The chill of the night air caught the young woman by surprise as she stumbled out of the club. A high-pitched whining noise reverberated in her head; its monotone shrill bounced around and added to the confusion she was already experiencing. The heat, mustiness and closeness in the club were fast replaced by a tingling chill that raised the hairs on her arms. Her sleeveless white top and denim miniskirt offered little warmth and protection.

Revellers poured out of the nightclub and chased down the odd taxi that sat in the cab rank. The young people jostled one another for a taxi, desperate to get out of the cold and head home to the comfort of their warm beds. In every direction from the club, people streamed away. Some headed to the late-night food takeaways to grab the mandatory burger or kebab to finish off the night in style.

Food was the last thing on her mind as she stood fixed to the spot. Her body swayed, and her eyes strained to focus in her drunken haze. With the tail-lights of the last remaining cab disappearing into town, she resigned herself to a journey home on foot. If she was lucky, she might be able to flag down a cab en route.

Her four-inch, black strappy heels pinched her feet. The clicking only aggravated her throbbing head as she walked, leaving behind the last remaining revellers. She headed in the vague direction of home, but in the darkness all the roads looked the same. She vaguely recognised the sign for the Premier Inn situated in North Street and staggered left down the dark side access road. She was certain that there was a small passage running alongside the NCP car park ahead of her.

Her head ached, and her body shook with the cold as she staggered left and fell against the wall. The cold brick felt rough against her fingers as her forehead came to rest on it.

Somewhere from behind her, she heard what sounded like a car pulling up. She wanted to turn and look, but her body refused to move, through a combination of fatigue and intoxication.

"Need a minicab, luv?" said the voice.

Her limp hand waved pathetically in the air. "Nooo, thanksh, I'm fiine..." she slurred. The orchestra in her head belted out its loudest tune and almost drowned out the sound of the car door opening and the footsteps approaching.

"You don't sound fine to me, luv. You need to get out of the cold. This is not the time or place to be walking around on your own. Anything could happen to you."

She waved the driver away. She knew what she wanted to say, but the words stuck in her throat.

He placed an arm around her shoulder another beneath her arm before guiding her towards the back door of his car.

"I'd never forgive myself if something happened to you. If you don't want me to drop you home, then at least let me drop you at the police station, and they can look after you," he said reassuringly.

She giggled as she fell into the seat. "Whoa, I think I've had a little...bit too much to drink. I'm feeling very...very shleepy," she said as she rested her head on the headrest. Her eyes felt heavy, her face felt numb. "Yessh, home."

The last thing she heard was a car door being closed and the familiar click of central locking.

She was sure she'd only closed her eyes for a few moments when the car came to a stop. Her head lolled back and forth, her drooping eyelids struggling to open.

"I'm just going to pop out and grab something," the man reassured her.

She waved dismissively at him as she pulled her phone from her clutch bag. She could see nothing but a white screen; the black digits were just a blur. "Yeahhh, whatever."

A gush of cold air rushed in when the car door opened. Her senses were jolted when someone grabbed her.

It all happened so quickly. She had no time to respond before someone placed a cloth over her face. She tried to pull the cloth away, but she had no strength. She felt more than fatigue now; every ounce of energy was evaporating at the same pace as a dark haziness enveloped her. Her eyes rolled back in her head as the sickly pungent smell on the cloth took hold.

SHE'S BEEN the easiest so far.

She'd practically fallen into his lap. The man was certain that she had taken the left turn deliberately because she wanted him to find her. She'd been waiting all evening to get him alone. The fact that she hadn't put up any resistance and had willingly come with him only confirmed that they were meant for each other.

What other reason was there for her not putting up a fight?

He dragged her unconscious body towards his unit. The excitement bubbled inside him as her strappy heels scraped on the floor. Her black-painted toenails poked out. He was tempted to stop right there and just worship her feet, but he would be patient. He knew she'd want him to be patient with her and take his time exploring her.

In the unit, he enjoyed every spine-tingling moment of slowly removing her sleeveless top and black lacy bra. Her breasts were large and firm. He smiled as he looked at the sizing label on her bra.

"36C, you *are* a big girl. You like the way I take my time? Well, I'm glad." He smiled at her as he continued his one-sided conversation. "I told you, Sally. She liked me. We can both enjoy her now."

With her flat on her back, he excitedly lifted the front of her short denim miniskirt. A low rumble rattled in his throat when he saw the woman's tiny black G-string nestled against her white flesh. He removed her last remaining garments and placed them neatly in a pile alongside her strappy shoes.

He stood back and admired her hourglass figure. Her large wholesome young breasts and clean-shaven pubic area held his gaze for what felt like an eternity. He undressed and lay next to her. Her red hair smelt fresh and intoxicating; he wrapped it around his fingers. Her skin felt smooth and inviting. He ran one finger in circles around her nipples. The delicate skin sent shivers of ecstasy coursing through his body.

"You're simply divine, another one of God's beautiful creations. I realised that you came to find me and Sally. You came to offer yourself to us."

His hooded gaze followed his fingers as they ran down the outside of her legs before tracing back up the inside where they met soft flesh. He groaned. His eyelids fluttered. His mind transported to a deep darkness of sexual gratification.

With a deft cut, he took a lock of her flame red hair and placed it inside a small silver trinket box.

Before wishing her good night, he wanted to make their connection deeper and stronger. She wanted it, he wanted it, and Sally wanted it.

He grabbed his knife and nicked the skin on her arm. Dark red velvety globules of blood burst to the surface. He admired how they clung together to form a dark exotic mass. She lay there, her eyes closed, inviting him to share in the most precious of life's commodities.

He licked her wound. Her blood tasted warm and sweet, just like her. An explosion of erotic intensity engulfed him, and his tongue hungrily searched out the last traces of her blood.

His fun ended for the moment. Sally wanted her to rest.

"You sleep well, my dearest. We'll have more fun soon," he said as he hauled her up and placed her inside the metal box, securing the lid with a padlock.

Now, I need to get rid of her phone.

23

Scott and Abby made their way the short distance towards the address for Mistress Claire. The drive gave him time to mull over the investigation. Abby had identified Yana Melnik as one of the women on the video footage seized from Freddie's bedroom, but she was a reluctant witness. Terrified of retribution and public humiliation, she had denied all requests from the police for a formal statement to confirm that the assailant in the video was Freddie. This frustrated Scott. He had a victim and evidence of a forced sexual assault, but pressing charges would be harder without the consent of the victim and a formal identification of the assailant.

He'd been clever to hide his identity on camera.

But Scott knew forensics had other ways of identifying images, like using body shape and identifiable features.

The knife, photographic and video evidence, and the items of female underwear had been sent away for forensic analysis. DNA analysis would no doubt confirm that the prints on the knife belonged to Freddie Coltrane and that his DNA would be found on the female underwear.

Scott's thoughts were interrupted by Abby's burst of laughter.

"What's so funny?" he asked as he kept his eye on the road ahead.

"Mistress Claire, the alternative lifestyle coach and fetish specialist," Abby read off her phone. "I'm an expert in domination, humiliation, BDSM and the treatment of submissives in general."

"Is this your other life outside of the job?"

"Ha ha, very funny."

"Never a dull moment in her life," Scott mused. "What more do we know about her?"

"She runs Brighton Dungeon. Her specialities are spanking, caning, flogging, whipping, humiliation and breath control – whatever that is."

She looked at Scott as she read out the next few points. "Check this out. Electrics, Ball busting...Trampling...Golden showers...Sploshing...And whatever else takes your fancy."

"This is supposed to be fun?" Scott said in bemusement. "I don't even know what half of those are."

"I do," Abby replied quickly as she furiously googled each one of those terms. "And at £160 per hour, I'm in the wrong business."

"And Freddie's been visiting her?"

Abby nodded in agreement with Scott's speculation. She pointed to the semi-detached house in Hove that was ahead of them and given as the address of Mistress Claire.

The house itself looked like all the other houses in this residential part of town. From the outside, there was nothing to suggest what really went on behind closed doors. As Scott knew from his days on the beat, there were men and women who paid large sums of money to explore their sexual boundaries. People who held down normal jobs and responsibilities by day, like office workers, doctors, solicitors, tradesmen, and housewives, sought dark, extreme pleasures by night.

An attractive, blonde, and busty woman answered the door. She wore a dark red fitted dress with a plunging neckline, and bright black painted stiletto heels.

She looked at both visitors at her door.

"Yes, can I help you?" she asked.

Scott and Abby held up their warrant cards for her to see. "I'm Detective Inspector Baker, and this is my colleague Detective Sergeant Trent, from Brighton CID. Are you Mistress Claire?"

The lady's eyes flicked from Scott to Abby before she gave their warrant cards a cursory glance and nodded to confirm her identity.

"May we come in and ask you a few questions?"

"Business or pleasure?" she asked Scott with a smile.

"We are here on business. We're making enquiries about a current investigation."

She showed them through to the lounge and invited them to take a seat.

The lounge was an opulent affair. Deep pile grey carpets matched the crushed grey velvet sofas. A large flat-screen TV sat above the fireplace, and various artistic prints adorned the walls.

"We'd like to ask you a few questions about a potential client. Freddie Coltrane," Scott said.

"Inspector, you must understand that I offer a discreet service. People come here because they trust me, and client confidentiality is something I promise all my clients."

Scott nodded. "I fully understand your situation, but we're in the middle of a murder investigation, and as a process of elimination, we're investigating everyone who may have had a connection with our victim."

Mistress Claire took a sharp intake of breath and placed a

hand on her chest. "Oh, dear, I'm sorry to hear that. Are you suggesting that Freddie Coltrane is complicit in some way?"

"I'm not at liberty to say either way," Scott said. "We're merely looking into his movements and all the people he has met. I understand he's a visitor here?"

Mistress Claire shook her head with concern. "I hope you don't think I've got anything to do with the murder or with Freddie Coltrane other than through my business?"

Scott confirmed once again that they were merely looking at Freddie Coltrane's movements and his lifestyle, which seemed to allay the woman's fears.

"Is this Freddie Coltrane?" Scott asked, holding up a picture.

Mistress Claire nodded. "Yes, that's him."

"Anything unusual about him and his preferences?" Scott asked.

The woman gave a hearty laugh. "Inspector, this is the place where most people come because they have the most *bizarre* and *perverse* preferences. There's nothing usual or unusual about the people who visit me. Let me show you."

Abby and Scott followed Mistress Claire down the hallway and through a door beneath the stairs. It appeared to lead down to her basement slash dungeon.

The room was a mixture of cosy relaxation and depravity. Dark red walls, low lighting and a vinyl floor stood in contrast to the soft bright red linen bed sheets on the four-poster bed to one side of the room. An intoxicating mix of fragrances wafted around the room, assaulting Scott's senses. Mistress Claire's heels clicked on the hard floor as she walked them around her domain.

"Is there anything that looks normal here?" she asked as she waved at the space.

Scott took his time as he wandered around, taking in the various tools and instruments of the woman's trade. A selection of whips, rubber straps and canes hung from one wall, which made his eyes pop. The table in one corner had an assortment of silver instruments, which Scott felt would be more at home in a hospital gynaecological unit. A wooden cross was pinned to one wall with a series of straps, which Scott assumed restrained clients by their wrists.

Mistress Claire watched Scott. "I have a pinwheel with little spikes that I roll over their body. Some people like it soft and find it very therapeutic. Others, on the other hand, enjoy the intense pain as it leaves a little trail of indentations."

"What's Freddie Coltrane into?" Scott asked.

"He likes a lot of marking, pain, and cuts. I do flog him quite a lot. He gets very excited when I draw blood. He likes a lot of CBT too."

Scott looked at her inquisitively.

Mistress Claire elaborated, saying, "It's a form of male genital torture."

"And that doesn't bother you?"

Mistress Claire shook her head and smiled. "Nothing fazes me, Inspector. Not when I have clients who want me to jab my six-inch heels into their nuts, or do a double barefoot stomp on their balls..."

Hearing those words made Scott wince. "And do you offer any other services?"

"If people can't come and see me in person but they want a reminder of me, they can also buy my stuff. I do a roaring trade in my used underwear."

Scott had heard it all. He shook his head in bewilderment. "Seriously?"

"Seriously, Inspector. People can buy my freshly worn knickers for thirty pounds. They tell me how long they'd like me to wear them for, and then I seal them in a bag and post it. They can buy my stockings, which I have worn for one day, for forty pounds."

"And who buys them, or is that a stupid question?" Abby asked.

"Loads of people. I especially get a lot of orders from the Far East and Saudi Arabia. The Japanese businessmen and the Saudi sheikhs have a real thing for blonde Englishwomen like myself."

They left Mistress Claire's, and Scott drove them back to the station.

"Well, that was an eye-opener," Abby remarked.

Scott couldn't help but agree. His thoughts turned to the information they had received about Freddie from Mistress Claire. It only reconfirmed their first assessment of Coltrane. He was clearly a man with extreme sexual tendencies who enjoyed humiliation, degradation, and pain.

Whilst in the basement, Scott had been out of mobile phone signal range. But as he drove, email and text messages started to come through.

One message from the station had Scott gripping the wheel tighter and sent shivers through his body.

24

The smell of engine oil hung in the air. It was the same familiar dirty smell of a mechanic's garage that everyone got when they walked into a car servicing garage to pick up their car. A concoction of dirty motor oil, chassis grease, brake dust, and solvent combined to create an aroma that clung to the walls and floor.

The chair creaked as the man leant back and rested his elbows on the armrests. His hands formed a steeple as he stared intently at the images on his laptop. Each image captured Rebecca's every movement, her every outline. The slimness of her figure contrasted heavily with the fullness of her chest that she tried in vain to hide beneath the leather jacket she wore everywhere.

He stopped at his favourite picture. It was of her leaving her house dressed in what he could only describe as a whore's outfit. A tight black miniskirt barely covered her creamy, white, firm thighs. Her black, long-sleeved blouse hugged her body, the buttons undone a little too low to be accidental. He'd smirked when he'd taken it.

He wondered what her parents would have thought had

they seen her, and whether they would have let her out dressed in next to nothing. Her outfit had been finished off with tacky thigh-high, black patent, high-heeled boots.

As she'd strutted down the road, she knew all eyes were on her. Men took a second glance; women cast disapproving scowls; cars slowed down; lorries and vans crawled while their male occupants shouted lewd comments.

Even the *man* sitting on the park bench in The Level noticed her – a dishevelled tramp holding out a white polystyrene cup, begging for any spare change. He'd kept the pound coin she'd given him. It had been a sign that she wanted him.

His eyes narrowed as he moved on to the next few images held in a folder marked 'Gym'. He'd trailed Rebecca many times from her home to the gym on London Road. He'd taken out a one-day pass on several occasions, to get closer. He'd loved watching her flex and stretch on the equipment. He had waited until she'd moved off on to another piece of equipment before sitting in the same place, relishing in the warmth she'd left on the seat.

It had taken every ounce of self-control to avoid getting aroused. Her tight, three-quarter-length leggings accentuated her firm legs and round, curvaceous backside. Her tight, sleeveless top clung to her sweaty chest. *Heaven*, he recalled saying to himself as he'd picked her discarded sweaty blue paper tissues out from the waste bin. It was something of hers that he could keep. It was her sweat, *her* moisture.

And here she was now, asleep behind him. He could hardly believe that she'd been attracted to him. That she'd accepted his offer of a lift.

"She's not as good as you, Sally. Then again, who is? But I'm glad you approve," he said.

Sally would always be his number one regardless of whom else he discovered. She'd been the only one to really understand him and his needs. She'd really got under his skin and figured him out. In his mind, they had created a connection that no one else had managed to do. From day one, Sally had said she'd always be by his side, and to this day, she'd been true to her word.

Through thick and thin, Sally had listened, reasoned, and supported him. Turned him into a better man. When others doubted, Sally didn't. When others abandoned him, Sally was there. When it felt like there was no hope for him and that he was a lost cause, Sally's unfaltering loyalty got him through those dark, troubled times. He'd hurt many people. His actions had been impulsive, irrational, and often uncontrollable, but Sally had been the calming influence he needed. Whenever he was with her, nothing else mattered.

In the beginning, he'd questioned Sally's motive many times.

Why me? Why spend hours every week with me in her office, when she can have any man she wants?

She was beautiful, caring, understanding, and attractive. She'd sit across from him as they chatted over a cup of tea. Her legs would be elegantly crossed, her sheer fine, flesh-coloured tights shimmering each time she moved. She had the grace of a swan, fluid in movement. Her gaze would lock onto him like a guided missile. Her warm, inviting smile reassured him. He felt safe with her.

Over the months they'd formed a bond, a relationship that felt exciting. She'd reassured him many times of her interest in him, and how she found him fascinating, almost intriguing.

Surely that meant she wanted him as much as he wanted her? He'd never really understood the notion of love. Everyone talked about it, and until he'd met Sally, he'd underrated all the fuss.

Sally had changed his opinion. He knew she loved him.

Why else would she say that she always looked forward to seeing him again as much as he looked forward to seeing her? He knew at that point that he could never live life without her. She might have disagreed when he suggested marriage, and the chance to move away and start a new life, but she'd finally relented. She'd given herself to him, falling for his charms, and fell into his arms.

Here they were now embarking on their journey together. Sally had insisted on him finding others to start a life with, people they could both enjoy. He could recall the exact moment Sally had said, "Nothing would make me happier than seeing you settled with another woman, and I look forward to meeting and getting to know her."

He had done just that.

Sadly, the women had never wanted to hang around for long. He'd found many that he was attracted to, but they always seemed to be missing qualities that rivalled Sally's.

He wasn't stupid, but the women thought he was. They thought he was a menace, dangerous even. He'd eliminated them when they became too much of a handful. After all, he couldn't risk them taking his intentions the wrong way and getting the police involved.

He turned towards Sally, saying, "I have to admit, this one seems to sleep a lot, my darling. I've tried to speak to her on several occasions, to get to know her, but she keeps her eyes closed and ignores me. What am I doing wrong? I've even nudged and poked her a few times, but she's being a stubborn bitch. I don't like it when people ignore me, do I, Sally?" He nodded in agreement with Sally's reply. "Yes, you're right, a typical lazy student."

He rose from his chair and stretched his aching muscles, his body stiff and tight. He'd lost count of the number of hours and days that he'd crouched on the many streets around Brighton, pretending to be homeless. He could never be like them. Filthy pond scum who spent the few pounds they'd begged for on cans of extra-strong beer or their next hit. They'd hang around in New Road by the Pavilion Gardens, sprawled out over the wooden benches, off their faces, while residents and tourists alike hurried past the intimidating sight.

He'd viciously scrubbed himself clean after every trip, his body red and raw in places from the nail brush he'd used and the disinfectant wipes.

He knelt by the box, the lid folded back to display his latest acquisition.

"You can't keep ignoring me forever, Rebecca. You'll have to open your eyes sooner or later," he said as he shook her shoulder. Her naked form still appealed to him even if her personality sucked.

He tutted at Rebecca's lack of response. "She's no fun, Sally. Reeks of booze. It's a rather unattractive quality. I'd like her to be awake so she can enjoy what I'm going to do to her."

He roughly grabbed one of her breasts, hoping that the change in approach would startle the unconscious woman, but his attempts were fruitless. He slapped her face in frustration.

He could at least sanitise her whilst she slept to save time.

He pulled out the first of many bleach wipes.

25

The report of a missing person rarely generated a large police response so soon after it had been reported unless it was a child or vulnerable person. Certain risk assessments would be carried out to identify if the person was really at risk. Questions would be asked about whether they had a history of going missing, any emotional or mental health issues and current domestic circumstances, and so on. Those first evaluations and enquiries would then allow the police to decide the level of risk and the relevant police response.

More than two hundred and fifty thousand people went missing in the UK every year. Sussex has had more than ten thousand go missing each year, and the police have neither the time nor the resources to fully investigate all the cases. The exceptions were for those who were deemed vulnerable or children. In such cases, the police response was large and fast.

This particular disappearance did require an immediate action, simply because it involved another student from Sussex University. The disappearance of two students in under a week raised a degree of alarm with both the university and the police officers investigating the cases.

Scott and Abby pulled up in Edinburgh Road. A local unit was already on scene, and Scott could see two uniformed officers doing door-to-door enquiries.

Abby exchanged a look of concern with Scott as she stepped through the doorway. Wooden splinters scattered the floor, but upon entering the lounge, none of the usual evidence suggested a burglary gone wrong.

A tall lanky man sat in one of the armchairs and rolled his mobile phone in his hand. Describing him as a man stretched the truth. He looked more like an overgrown youth, with long spindly arms and legs, a white T-shirt that hung off his thin frame, and faded, ripped jeans. His face still bore the last remnants of bad teenage acne; dark red angry spots peppered his pale complexion.

Mike was the first CID officer on the scene and had just completed taking notes when Abby and Scott entered.

"This is Andy Barton, guv," Mike said, thumbing in the direction of the lad. "He's the one who reported the young woman missing. There's another female and male student that share this property. Rebecca Thorne, Becky to her friends, went out partying last night in town. She never returned. No one's heard from her, guv."

Scott glanced around the room. It was reminiscent of the student digs that he used to live in, littered with a mixture of odd sofas, coffee tables and ornaments that looked as if they'd come from separate lounges and been thrown into this one room.

"Presumably they've tried her phone?"

"Yes, guv. It goes straight to voicemail."

Scott turned towards Barton. There were no worry lines or nervous behaviour from him. Scott knew that students often bunked down on each other's floors at short notice after a heavy night out. Some would find themselves waking up the following morning beside a stranger with an embarrassing, remorseful headache and a vague recollection from the night before.

"Has Rebecca done anything like this before?" Scott asked Barton.

The lanky kid shrugged and shook his head. "Not since I've known her. We all moved into this house in September last year, and it's not like her to stay out all night without telling us." He paused for a moment before continuing, "And with all that stuff going on up at campus...and then Hailey..."

Scott could hear the awkwardness in the boy's voice. He had done the right thing in reporting his flatmate missing.

Scott nodded at the front door. "What happened?"

"We were broken into, but the strange thing is nothing was taken."

"And how do we know she is not in a lecture?"

"Because our other flatmate, Lacey Manners, is in the same class as her. She's in class now, and Rebecca hasn't turned up."

Mike continued to fill Scott in with his brief notes from the interview. "She went to the Coalition nightclub last night in the King's Road Arches. She's been often and has always returned from a night out there. That's why Andy thinks it's a bit out of character for her."

"Abby, can you get Raj to head over to confirm she was there, and check CCTV both from outside and inside the club. Hopefully one of the cameras might have caught her."

Abby left the room to make her call.

"Okay, Andy. Thanks for your help so far. Can you stay here in case we need to talk to you again?"

Andy shrugged and sauntered out of the room, his long thin arms swaying like long branches of a tree caught in the wind.

Scott had received an email update from Meadows. The super had pointed out that the vice chancellor of the university was concerned and had issued an email warning reminding students to remain vigilant and be extra cautious with their safety.

An earlier message from Helen had confirmed no recent sightings of Freddie Coltrane despite an extensive search of the lecture theatres and the East Slope area. Scott fired off a reply to Helen, asking her to track down Lacey Manners and gather more information on Rebecca.

"What was she studying, Mike?" Scott asked as Abby rejoined them.

"Geography," Mike replied and handed Scott a recent photograph of Rebecca Thorne.

The image of Rebecca raised alarm bells in Scott's head.

She had a pale complexion, dark brooding eyes and an attractive figure. But it wasn't her figure that caused his belly to pinch with anxiousness. It was her long flowing tresses and curls of hair that cascaded over her shoulders and down her front.

Abby was looking over Scott's shoulder. "Another redhead. Coincidence?"

Scott knew it was anything but a coincidence.

26

Back at the station, Scott's mind swirled as he waited by the coffee machine for his cappuccino. Abby's observation about Rebecca's hair colour played on his thoughts. It wasn't uncommon for killers to find victims with similar traits or characteristics. Equally, some victims had little similarity between each other and were killed purely for the thrill and satisfaction.

Scott's phone vibrated in his pocket. A quick glance at the screen told him that Meadows wanted a quick word with him in his office. Scott groaned. He had enough on his plate without another lecture from Meadows.

With a hot plastic cup of something that resembled a cappuccino in one hand and his notepad in the other, Scott strode into Meadows's office.

The sharp jolt of his body splashed some of his cappuccino over his hand. Scott's eyes flicked between Meadows, who was leaning back in his chair, and the smartly dressed female sitting in the opposite chair.

Scott's mind struggled to process the shock he felt. He hadn't seen this face in a few years, and now every muscle in his body tensed in apprehension. A mixture of dread and anger coursed through his veins.

"Ah, Scott, good of you to join us so quickly. I wasn't sure if you were in the building," Meadows said, nodding at the spare seat.

Scott sat and breathed in and out, desperate to control his racing heart, afraid that he would give away the anxiety that was turning the insides of his stomach like a tombola wheel.

Meadows's eyes flicked between Scott and the visitor. A wry smile threatened to break through the practised sternness of his face. "Scott, you remember DCI Berry from Essex Police?" Meadows gave the female visitor a warm smile.

Detective Chief Inspector Hermione Berry sat with her slender legs crossed, slowly sipping a cup of tea. Her shiny, dark brown hair hung long over her shoulders and framed her round face and tight jawline. She looked the consummate professional in her navy two-piece suit and white blouse. Her dark brown eyes lit up in the way they would when two old friends met after a long time.

She beamed a large, welcoming smile. "Hello, Scott. It's been a long time. Detective Superintendent Meadows has been filling me in on what a valuable asset you've been to CID here."

Her words held a degree of sincerity, but Scott knew she was only responding to the specific things that Meadows had told her.

Scott could only muster a small nod in DCI Berry's direction. His next words had stuck in his throat.

Meadows said, "Scott, the case that you're working on at the moment has come to the attention of Essex Police, and in particular DCI Berry. It was the DCI's personal request to be seconded to our team to work on this case. Essex worked on a series of similar unsolved cases five years ago in Colchester and the surrounding areas of Essex."

His superior's words bounced off Scott as he sat there in stunned silence. He could see Meadows's lips move, but Scott's mind had muted the sound.

Meadows gave Berry an enquiring nod to confirm that he had the right details. Berry nodded in agreement. He then continued to update Scott with more background information to the Essex cases.

"There was a series of similar cases that involved victims who were students from the University of Essex. Jackie Stickley and Alison Gray were both abducted and murdered within weeks of each other. The MO matches that of Hailey Bratton. Both victims were redheads and mutilated in the same way."

Meadows paused, and DCI Berry continued. She cleared her throat. "Unfortunately, we drew a blank with suspects, and the killer was never identified. It became a cold case after that." She shrugged.

Scott sat rigid and pulled his shoulders back. "Sir, ma'am, I appreciate the similarities in the cases and the offer of help, but with the Essex case files being cold, surely it makes sense for us to keep pushing with our live cases and keep Essex Police in the loop. I'm sure we are more than capable."

"I'm sure you're right, Scott, but the decision for Essex and Sussex Police to work together has been agreed by AC Grayling and CC Lennon," Meadows said. "They are fully supportive of the collaboration between our two forces." He paused before directing his next words at Scott. "We've organised a press conference tomorrow where myself and DCI Berry will go public with this case. It will also give the general public the reassurance they need and might serve to jog a few memories in relation to the cold cases."

In principle he was fine with that, but DCI Berry presented a major problem for him.

Meadows leant forward in his chair as if about to divulge

some secret that only the three of them would be privy to. "I understand you both know each other and have worked together, so the sharing of knowledge should be much easier. I'm sure you'll be able to get the DCI up to speed very quickly, Scott."

27

Scott headed back to his office and paced the worn floor like a caged lion. His jaw was clenched tight, his lips pursed in a thin line, and his eyes fixed wide in bewilderment.

DCI Berry had followed him into his office. "I know this is probably a shock, Scott. When I heard about the case and the second disappearance, I just had this feeling that whoever had committed our unsolved murders was more than likely responsible for Hailey's death."

Scott resisted the temptation to say something he might later regret. He drew on every ounce of self-control to push that red mist to one side. He crossed his arms, willing at least to listen.

"Yes, we could have discussed the cases and their relevance over the phone," she continued. "But I never nicked the sicko who did this to Jackie Stickley and Alison Gray. I'm good at my job, and having those two cold cases sitting against my name doesn't make me feel good. I want to find the bastard who did this to those girls, and I won't give up until I find him. Surely it makes sense for us to pool our resources and intelligence on these cases? With a bit of luck, we can get some brownie points both in Essex and Sussex."

Scott begrudgingly accepted that she had a valid point. What frustrated him was the fact that again Meadows hadn't consulted him. To rub more salt in the wound, there had been no mention of him attending the press conference tomorrow either.

Scott left his office, and Berry kept step with him.

The team looked up in surprise and exchanged inquisitive looks as the pair walked towards them.

"Team, can I have your attention?" Scott asked. "I'd like to introduce you to DCI Hermione Berry from Essex Police. She's requested a secondment to our team to help us with our ongoing investigations into the murder of Hailey Bratton and the potential disappearance of Rebecca Thorne. DCI Berry will now fill you in on the reasons that she's here."

Scott took one step back and stuffed his hands in his pockets. DCI Berry gave him a nod.

"Thank you, Scott. I know you're probably surprised that I've just turned up, and that you weren't warned about it. I apologise for that, as I do to DI Baker because he wasn't aware of it either." She glanced at Scott and gave him a sweet smile.

Berry walked over to the incident board and put up two extra pictures of Jackie Stickley and Alison Gray. "These are two victims who were murdered more than five years ago. Both were students at the University of Essex, and both were redheads. They were aged between eighteen and twenty; they had no earlier records and were just your average students. They were abducted, mutilated, and murdered within weeks of each other. We still have no motive for the murders. The only things in common were that they were students and both redheads."

The team's attention remained fixed on the images, but Abby's eyes were firmly fixed on Scott.

"DC Mike Wilson," Mike announced. "Do you have any theories, ma'am, as to why it has been more than five years between your murders and ours?"

Berry turned towards Mike. "Good to meet you, Mike. Unfortunately, we have no idea as to why if this is the same person. The person may have been banged up and has only recently been released and went on to reoffend. And obviously, that's a line of enquiry we definitely need to follow. They may have just been away or working abroad and have only just returned. But that's just speculation and potential reasons why. But it's not uncommon for killers to go underground for a bit, then commit these acts when something in their life triggers them to reoffend."

Mike nodded and raised an eyebrow. "Are we ruling out Freddie Coltrane, then? He wouldn't have been old enough to be responsible for the Essex cases."

"If we're going down the road of redheads and students being the common link, then perhaps. But we can't rule out the possibility of it being a copycat killer." Scott sighed.

DCI Berry grabbed her notepad and pen from the desk beside her. "Okay. So what I'll do is sit down with you individually and just get up to speed with what you've been doing. I need to see what lines of enquiry you are following and what evidence we've managed to gather so far. Is that okay with you, Scott?"

Scott nodded before he turned and headed off. He shouted over his shoulder to no one in particular, "I'll be in my office if you need me."

He sat down heavily in his chair and blew out his cheeks. Tiredness washed over him. His legs felt like lead weights, and his eyelids felt like they were attached to two bags of sand. He needed a coffee and some chocolate to boost his energy levels. He opened his top drawer and spotted a Cadbury Flake. It was only then that he realised he hadn't eaten today.

No wonder I feel like a sack of shit.

Abby appeared in his doorway. His moment of pleasure would have to wait a few more seconds. She leant against the frame and tilted her head. "You okay, guv?"

Scott ran his hand through his hair and closed his eyes.

Eventually he nodded. "Yes, I'm fine. I've just got a lot on my plate at the moment. You know how it is, stacks of paperwork, case files to review, management reports. Do I need to continue?" He groaned and continued, "Listen, I know you've talked about going for DI, but trust me, sometimes it's not worth the extra aggravation."

Abby raised her brow in suspicion. "It's me you're talking to. Either you're not happy about the DCI being dumped on your lap, or you're not happy about Meadows interfering again."

Scott laughed softly. "Nothing gets past you, Sherlock, does it?"

"I'm still waiting," Abby said as she crossed her arms in defiance. "Do you know much about DCI Berry?"

Scott closed his eyes again, knowing that if he opened them, Abby would see straight through his next fabrication.

He shook his head. "I know of her, but I don't really know much about her. She was based in another part of Essex." He hoped that it would be enough to get Abby off his back.

Abby nodded slowly, clearly unconvinced, and walked out.

28

The darkness of the room matched the blackness of the man's mood. He'd always looked forward to his weekly therapy sessions with Sally, but more recently she had taken on an air of arrogance and assertiveness with him that he didn't like.

Nevertheless, a part of him always looked forward to seeing her.

She understood him.

Agreed with him.

Pacified him.

He sat in the solitary chair by the desk as he gazed at the reflection in the full-length mirror beyond. The mirror showed a man smartly dressed in a dark grey suit that made him look professional, senior and authoritative. His crisp white shirt added boldness to his statement, the colour in marked contrast to the gloom that surrounded him. A smart red silk tie completed the ensemble.

He took a small sip of tea from the china cup before putting it back down on the saucer. It was strong and dark, just the way he liked it. He'd never quite understood why people always insisted on having milky tea. When it was full-fat milk, the gloopy liquid often clung to the insides of his mouth.

He glanced at his environment; the office wasn't how he remembered it. Things were certainly going downhill, in his opinion. He glanced at himself in the mirror a second time and raised an eyebrow in dissatisfaction. Confusion clouded his thoughts. He couldn't quite understand why Sally had swapped the aroma of lavender from her diffuser for engine oil. It was anything but soothing.

"How am I?" he asked as he looked into the eyes of the reflection.

"I'm very well, thank you. A few aches and pains, but I can't grumble," he offered. "Yes, I'm pleased to be here, too. It's been a tough time, but with your guiding hand, I've never felt better." He gave a wry smile.

Then he nodded a few times as he listened to the voice reply in his head. She had a calming, plum voice, her every syllable pronounced with perfection. She was a woman with a mystical presence who whisked him away to the deepest, safest part of his mind.

A satisfied smile spread across his face as he hung on her every word.

There she goes again, working her hypnotic charms on me, wrapping me in words that spring straight out of a dictionary. Verbigeration, I love that word. She always says I do a lot of that. And if she says I do that a lot, then that's clearly something to be proud of.

He felt smug, content even, that she was impressed by his range of vocabulary.

He shook his head. "No, I don't need those pills anymore. I was given them to take, and yes, they were helpful to begin with, but I've changed now. I'm in control of my moods and behaviour. Surely you can see it yourself?"

He stared long and hard at the mirror, waiting for a response. Perhaps she was doing the 'silent' thing that she so often did to get him to open up.

A chill gripped the room as the evening wore on. The hairs on the back of his neck bristled as he listened harder. A deep laugh echoed around the large empty space. "As the saying goes, physically I'm here, mentally I'm far, far away." Then his smile disappeared as he brought his attention back to the reflection.

His eyes danced across the mirror. "I'm like any other man." He pointed a finger at his reflection. "It's been a long time since I've done those things. I wouldn't harm anyone now. I've seen the error of my ways. Now I prefer my own company, a glass of wine and a good book."

He wasn't going to lie down and take being called heartless and lacking in remorse. Blood surged through his veins, and his temples throbbed.

"I'm not an animal," he growled through clenched teeth. "I'm not going to let them get away with it, am I? If someone pisses me off, then I have to let them know."

Anger spewed from every pore. His cheeks became red and blotchy.

He picked up his cup and saucer and threw them across the room. "You're not listening! I've changed! I can't help it if they make me angry."

He soothed the reflection. "Listen...I am not what happened to me. I am what I choose to be." He drew in a deep breath and waited for the adrenaline to subside.

His hands trembled as he sat back down.

The reflection remained still, neither unmoved nor perturbed by his outburst.

A noise from behind him interrupted the man. Heavy thuds and muffled screams punctured the silence, testing his patience. He looked up at the dark ceiling, praying for the silence to return.

He looked back at the reflection. "I'm sorry for the rude interruption. Workmen. You know how it is? Insensitive and useless bastards at the best of times."

29

Rebecca Thorne's head spun. She tried to focus in the darkness, but despite attempts to blink the sleep away, blackness still engulfed her.

She pushed hard against the confines of the metal box. The cold metal chilled the soles of her feet. Waves of panic rolled through her, pricking her skin, causing sweat to form on her forehead. Despite the coldness of her environment, her body felt hot and tacky.

Random images and flashbacks of memories rushed through her mind. She recalled the blurry images of revellers who had passed her by, and street lights that had flickered in slow motion. Then there had been this sudden warmth of familiarity, the interior of a car. And that was where her recollections faded. Nothing after that memory made sense. In fact, none of it made sense.

With the little energy she had left, she pushed and thrashed against the sides of the container. She thumped the side of her fist on the cold metal. "Help!" her voice croaked.

Part of her mind sprang into action when the box rattled. Bright light dazzled her vision. A white orb caused her eyes to sting. She lifted her hands to shield them from the burning sensation. Another stinging sensation shocked her. She jerked back from the repeated slaps to her cheek and the burning warmth that was fast spreading.

He stared at her naked form for a few minutes, fascinated by the rapid rise and fall of her chest. He'd almost forgotten just how magnificent she looked naked. Her breasts, still young and pert, defied gravity. Her nipples stood hard against the rush of cold air that raced across her glistening body. He ran his finger across her moist navel, then tasted the saltiness.

He smiled. "Rebecca, you really do choose your moments. I was in a really important meeting, and you spoilt it. And yes, I admit I was angry, but looking at you now, how can I be angry at such a beauty? You were trying to get my attention. But you don't have to play games with me because you've already got my attention. You've already won my heart."

He leant forward and touched her, probed her in places that made her flinch and squirm away from him. He watched as her lids flickered and closed, and her body fell limp.

"Now, now, Rebecca, I don't want you to go too soon. It would be nice if you hung around a bit longer than the last one. We're only just getting to know one another, and I've got so much to tell you. You really are a beauty lying here naked, inviting me to explore you."

He unscrewed the lid from the Lucozade bottle and lifted her head. He fed her sip by sip.

"You'll feel much better after this," he reassured her. "It's a good thing that you had your diabetic ID bracelet in your bag."

30

The station canteen offered a sanctuary to tired and weary officers coming to the end of a long day shift or who were just about to start the night shift. Several uniformed officers sat in small huddles, sipping on cups of tea and coffee, quiet murmurs occasionally punctured by hearty laughs.

Raj sat flicking through a copy of the local *Argus* newspaper. The pages offered the usual mix of news that seemed to fill the newspaper these days. Various reports of motor vehicle accidents peppered the pages, along with articles relating to numerous arrests and the rundown of festivals that were happening up and down Brighton and Hove. He wasn't into sport, so he tended to skip the last few pages.

He shook his head as he read an article about how a shoplifter had racially abused a shop assistant. Raj recognised the local Co-op in Western Road. He scanned through the article. It went into detail about how the shoplifter picked items off the shelf and put them into his bag. When challenged at the checkout, he verbally abused staff and grabbed a security guard by the chest before being restrained.

It wasn't the story that bothered him but the reference to the racially abusive language that had been directed towards the shop assistant. It was this aspect of the crime that incensed Raj and challenged his beliefs about humanity and society.

Being an Asian officer, he had attracted more than his fair share of racially abusive comments while arresting suspects. It was something that came with the territory, and something that he had got used to. As a young PC working Friday and Saturday nights, he had been spat at, assaulted and had racial taunts thrown at him. To begin with, he had found them both hurtful and demoralising. As time went by, and with the support of his fellow officers, he had learnt to accept the abuse.

It was something he'd experienced his whole life. At secondary school, he was one of only five Asian pupils in his academic year. Racial taunts and physical abuse were an unfortunate accepted norm of school life. He had spent many a night wishing that he had been born white like his fellow school friends so that he could blend into his environment and feel normal.

"Penny for your thoughts?"

Raj jolted and looked up from his newspaper. DCI Berry was standing there with two cups. She held one out. "I hope you like tea?"

Raj shifted uncomfortably. "Yes...erm, yes, ma'am," he said.

DCI Berry pulled out the chair opposite Raj; the metal legs screeched on the floor. "I hope you don't mind me joining you?"

Raj straightened up more and checked to make sure that his tie and top button were done up. Berry looked just as immaculate after a full shift as she had that morning. Her hair was smooth and shiny. Her suit looked neatly ironed, and her white blouse appeared crease-free. She had the poise and elegance of a corporate professional, and the attractiveness only a confident woman can exude.

He cleared his throat. "No, not at all, ma'am. I was just reading the paper, but nothing of interest. I thought I'd grab a quick break."

Berry nodded. "I try to avoid the papers myself. I think we deal with enough crap without being reminded of it."

"You're not wrong there, ma'am."

"Are you enjoying the job?"

Berry's question took Raj by surprise. Her tone hinted of subterfuge. Or perhaps that was just him being super cautious because of her seniority.

"Yes, ma'am. I love the job. It's all I've ever wanted to be. Even more so because I'm Asian."

Berry raised an eyebrow.

Raj continued, feeling the need to explain himself, "Whilst growing up, there was always an air of suspicion around the police, especially among the minority communities. I had loads of friends who didn't like the police. You know, the usual stuff, the continuous stop and search, the them-versus-us mentality, and of course the...*institutionalised racism*." Raj emphasised the last few words as he levelled his cautious gaze at Berry, not sure how she would take it.

Berry nodded, her face giving nothing away. "Well, we're glad that you've chosen this career, and hopefully you've set a great example to many in your community."

Raj nodded and accepted that as a genuine comment.

Berry stirred her tea. "And how do you find working for DI Baker?"

The question was casual; Berry's eyes remained firmly fixed on her drink.

Raj pondered her question for a few moments. "He's the

best guv I've worked for. He listens to all of us. He's down-to-earth, and he's always got our back."

Berry gave an approving nod. "That's good to know. I always knew he would do well. It's good to know that he's got your back. How did you all cope with Sian's death, then?"

"We all took it hard. Sian was a great officer and a good friend," Raj replied and cleared his throat. "Her loss shook us all. One minute she was here, and the next..." He trailed off and looked down.

"And how did DI Baker take it?"

Raj looked up, locking his gaze on Berry. Her innocent questions were starting to sound probing. Her face was expressionless, but her eyes were alert.

"As I said, we all took it really hard, including the guv. I think he felt personally responsible."

"And was he...personally responsible?"

Raj's eyes narrowed at the accusation.

He clenched his teeth and shook his head. "No, ma'am, he wasn't. What happened to Sian could have happened to any officer anywhere in the country. It's a risk we all accept when we clock in every day."

"And is that how every officer in the station sees it?"

"You'd have to ask them, ma'am. I'm just expressing my point of view."

DCI Berry pushed her chair back. She paused for a moment, as though reflecting on Raj's comment.

"It's been good talking to you, Raj. I like getting to know the officers that I'm working with. It helps to build that level of trust and working partnership that we need to do our jobs properly and get the results we're looking for. I'm going to head off now, but if there's anything you want to talk about, then my door is always open."

Raj nodded and watched Berry as she strode purposefully out of the canteen. A feeling of unease rippled through him.

31

Scott drained the last remains of his cold coffee. He'd been meaning to top it up with a fresh refill, but time had just flown by staring at his computer screen. With a grimace, he tongued the bitter coffee taste coating the inside of his mouth. He pushed his cup to one side, cursing his decision to finish it off.

He drew his hands down his face and stared up at the ceiling. The team had all gone home except for Raj, who had the late shift. Scott felt tired, and his body ached. He needed his bed, but the case was playing too much on his mind.

Sometimes a case flowed smoothly, with a good spread of witnesses, forensic evidence or CCTV footage. Gathering all the information helped to either confirm the timeline of events leading up to a crime, or at least give them active lines of enquiry. But this case appeared more complicated. Motives regarding the abduction and murder of Hailey Bratton were unclear, but with the second abduction and a link to historical cases in Essex, a possible trend was now being mooted around.

Scott relied on his trusted notepad rather than the incident board as he sketched out his thoughts. He'd drawn a line down the centre. On one side he'd written Hailey Bratton, and on the other side, Rebecca Thorne. As far as he could see, they had nothing in common other than both being redheads and attending the same university. They didn't share the same social circle or play the same sports or even have similar interests.

He circled Rebecca's name several times and decided that her background needed further investigation.

Scott's mind drifted back to DCI Berry and her unexpected presence in Meadows's office. He gritted his teeth as he reflected on how his past had a knack of screwing up his happiness. No matter what he did, events from the past seemed to not only haunt him but pop up when he least expected it.

It wasn't even a relationship that he and Berry had shared. It had been less than that. A drunken mistake that had led to a trail of deceit and blackmail. It hadn't taken him long to realise that DCI Berry was a self-absorbed, manipulative officer whose only goal was self-preservation, but by then the damage had already been done.

Scott blinked hard and sat up straight, bringing him back to the present.

The press appeal about Hailey and Rebecca that Scott had organised ahead of Meadows's formal press conference had yielded lots of calls, and for that he was grateful. Now the laborious task began of sifting through every call and ranking them in level of importance from low to medium and high. The calls that were ranked as high or medium would be investigated and followed up first, as their time was limited and so were their resources.

One call had been of particular interest to the team. It had related to a possible unlicensed taxi touting for trade. That in itself wasn't an odd occurrence in and around town –

the public was regularly warned about the dangers of getting into an unlicensed taxi. But it was the fact that several calls had come from women who had all reported the same issue. They all described one particular driver as creepy, in his mid-forties and dressed smartly in a suit.

DCI Berry appeared in his doorway. Scott jolted in his chair.

"Sorry, ma'am, I didn't realise you were there."

DCI Berry smiled and leant against the frame of the door with her arms folded. "I didn't want to disturb you. I know what you're like when you're deep in thought. You number crunch, go through a thousand different hypotheses in your mind, and generally switch off from the world around you."

Berry's assessment of him was pretty much spot on. It would take a herd of buffalo to distract him when he was knee-deep in a tough case.

"I'm just going through the cases and trying to find other links between Hailey and Rebecca –if indeed any exist. I know it's early days, but we are following several lines of enquiry, including reports about a suspicious taxi driver who's been approaching women. I've instructed the control room to liaise with the CCTV team in town and see if we can find this unlicensed cab on any of the footage, and we're looking at phone and GPS data for both girls."

Berry nodded in agreement. "Stating the obvious, but I think being a redhead has something to do with it. When I dealt with the Essex job, we identified eleven cases in which women with red hair had either gone missing or had been murdered in the past five years. We ran dozens of checks on their backgrounds to try to find a commonality, or some link other than being a redhead, but we drew a blank." She sounded frustrated.

"And did you arrive at the conclusion that all eleven cases *were* connected?"

"Some were, in terms of students and being redheads. Others appeared more random. But in our opinion, they were all linked because of the way in which they were finally murdered." Berry drew her finger across her navel, to indicate the manner in which they had been cut.

Scott flipped open a brown folder on his desk and thumbed through the pieces of paper. He pulled out one particular sheet and waved it in the air for Berry to take.

She did.

Scott said, "Matt Allan, our guy from forensics, came back on the oil traces that were found on the heels of victim one. It has a unique composition. It's used in marine engineering. I think he referred to it as break-in oil. It's not used now. It has a high concentration of metallic debris."

When Berry looked blankly at him, he continued, "Don't ask me when, but before the advent of new marine technology, engines were factory-filled with a special oil. This oil contained an extra dose of detergent and other additives that helped new engine parts, especially bearings and piston rings, to wear in together. The metallic debris from this 'break in' would be carried away by the break-in oil and flushed from the engine on that first oil change."

"And they don't do that anymore?"

"Not as far as I know. Things have moved on since then. But the point is Hailey Bratton had been somewhere where there was evidence of this marine oil."

"Places where the engines were made, perhaps?"

"Or where they were repaired," Scott said, pointing at her with his pen.

Berry rocked on her feet in consideration.

Scott added, "And just before you say, Matt has identified nineteen locations along the south coast that were industries or trades associated with marine engineering. That's going to be our next line of investigation first thing tomorrow morning."

"I'm impressed, Scott. You're not just a pretty face. But then I've always known that, haven't I?" Berry winked and smiled.

Scott offered a weak smile. If someone else had said that to him, he would have laughed at the joke. For Berry to say it, she was teasing him, which riled him once again.

He stared at her. "Why are you really here? We could have done all of this over the phone."

"I thought that would be clear, Scott," she replied, raising a brow. "The chance to crack a case possibly spanning two counties...and seeing you again." She let her words hang in the air before she turned and walked off.

Silence enveloped Scott once again. A cold stillness hung in the air. Berry had always been an elusive character, and that made Scott wary. Their connection had gone beyond professional when he was in Essex police, a situation that he'd regretted ever since. And now she was back. For what reason, he wasn't entirely sure. Yes, she wanted to lend a hand with his case and in turn perhaps solve her cold cases. But with Berry, Scott knew there was always a hidden agenda.

Scott got up and looked out of his window into the blackness of the night. Most of the town might be asleep, but his mind wouldn't switch off.

He checked his watch. He'd promised Cara that he would be home for dinner. But the hours had passed, and he was buried knee-deep in paperwork. He had reluctantly sent her a text telling her he was stuck in the office. He felt guilty for letting Cara down, and he had heard the disappointment in her voice when she'd phoned shortly after receiving his text message.

32

Freddie rang once on the doorbell and waited patiently, glancing up and down the quiet suburban street. For company that evening he had the nightly predators – owls, foxes and rats that scurried from garden to garden, searching for morsels of food and tiny insects.

The key turned in the door, then opened, revealing a low-lit hallway. The only illumination came from a small table lamp emitting a red glow that barely made things any clearer.

Mistress Claire stood there, a dark and red silhouette in the light. Her black crotchless PVC catsuit squeaked as she walked.

Words were unspoken between them. They knew the drill. She led him by the hand down the hallway and into the basement.

THE LEATHER CUT into his wrists as he lay spreadeagled and naked on the table. A broad, eager smile spread across his face in anticipation of what was to come.

Each whip of the leather paddle on his erect penis sent shivers of ecstatic pain through his body. He clenched his bound hands and curled his toes as he fought and failed to protect his body from the repeated strikes. His eyes rolled back in his head as his mind escaped to the darkest of places.

"I've been a bad boy, mistress."

"How bad?"

"Real bad, I've been greedy –" His words were cut off when electricity coursed through his skin via the electrodes attached to his nipples. With each click of the dial, the mistress exacted the pain he truly deserved.

Sweat beaded on his forehead. "Yesss," Freddie hissed through gritted teeth.

She firmly gripped the shaft of his penis and slid the cold metal pin through the tip and into his urethra. He squirmed and thrashed when a burning bolt of pain erupted in his groin. His eyes widened in a mixture of terror and hedonism as she slowly pulled it out.

His constant thrashing needed to be tempered, he knew that. Several hard slaps across both cheeks from her left a trail of burning pain on his face.

Freddie screamed.

"Silence!" she barked. "I'm in charge here. You will scream when I tell you to scream. You will move when I tell you to move, understood?" She pushed the steel rod in farther.

"Yes, mistress." He groaned, nodding as his eyes widened more.

The mistress took her time punishing him. He had paid for an hour, and she would make sure he got what he'd asked for. What he needed. She was the consummate professional, well experienced in her trade. She judged the quality of her work by the level of pain and discomfort she meted out to her customers.

"Hurt me. Mark me," he whispered.

The mistress took one of the many candles that flickered around the room and held it above his chest. He gasped in anticipation, his muscles rigid, ready to receive the next round of punishment. His back arched when the first drops of molten candle wax fell on his chest. No sooner had they dried, new drops fell along the length of his chest and abdomen. Waxy, white trails hardened and pulled his skin tight.

Freddie groaned as his body loosened to the pleasure.

Now he was spent.

"I should have brought Hailey here to you. You could have done a better job than me."

"You're more than welcome to bring the next one to me," the mistress replied as she untied his bindings and flipped him over onto his front.

He gripped the handrails on either side of the table. He knew what came next. He wasn't sure if he noticed the crack of the whip first or the searing heat of the laceration on his back. He arched his back as repeated strokes bore down on him like hailstones. She showed him no leniency or compassion.

Each strike cut deeper and deeper into his skin. His teeth were now firmly clenched tight as his body fought to numb the pain. He needed this. He had done bad things and needed the punishment. He needed to experience the pain that he had inflicted on so many others.

A deep, guttural scream bubbled up and caught in his throat. What felt like a series of acupuncture needles punctured a line across his back. Each tiny hole made by the spiked wheel drew a red globule of blood that formed the dotted trail. Every part of him wanted to cry out, but he knew the risks of doing so.

Oh, how he enjoyed his visits here. They pandered to his

deepest desires. Desires that he kept locked safely in his mind, only explored when he found a suitable woman to help him release them. He'd tried exploring his darkest fantasies with Hailey, but she had been too prudish for him. She had told him that she would do anything for him because she loved him so much, but she never did. She never lived up to her side of the bargain. She had been all talk and no action.

A momentary lapse in the mistress's onslaught gave him a few precious moments to recover. His racing heart pounded against his ribs whilst she got up upon the table to stand astride him.

The final act of humiliation was the one he liked best and often asked her to keep until the end.

A warm liquid trickled onto his back and stung the redness, the welts, and cuts. Her golden shower always made his visit complete.

33

A gleeful smile of self-satisfaction spread across the man's face as he leant back in his chair. He was in complete control. He had kept Rebecca teetering on the edge. Just when it looked like all hope was fading in her eyes, he'd come to her rescue, like a knight in shining armour.

He delighted when her eyes shone with gratitude for him. The way in which her soulful eyes had looked at him made him feel special. When those around her were letting her down, he was there to support her, to be there in her hour of need. She hadn't said it in those words, but he could tell by her expression that she loved him.

He scanned various photographs on his laptop. He had created a new folder with new images. If there was one thing he liked about his job, it was the freedom to explore the length and breadth of the town in search of beautiful women. Of course, they never saw *him* because he had perfected the art of blending in with his surroundings. He never wore anything garish, anything loud or bright that would attract attention. He usually stuck to neutral colours like black or white T-shirts, dark jeans or trousers and dark hoodies. Darker clothes proved particularly helpful at night when he could move in the shadows.

"I agree, Sally," he said with a nod of his head. "We would like Rebecca to stay with us as long as possible, and the thought of her being alone doesn't sit comfortably with me. Your suggestion of finding her a friend is a perfect idea. A playmate. There's nothing better than two females locked and entwined in a passionate, exciting embrace."

The prospect of holding two young vibrant women captive excited him. His heart began to pound too fast, threatening to burst from his chest. The hairs on the back of his neck bristled. His groin ached from deep within. His mind raced ahead as various visions cascaded over each other, each new one more exciting than the last.

"You know me too well, Sally. I know, I know, you don't need to keep reminding me about how I get carried away. What can I say? I'm getting greedy."

He rubbed his hands in excitement and puckered his lips as he pulled his chair closer to his desk and leant over his laptop. He had captured so much content; he barely knew where to start.

He was always like this when he was about to start a new endeavour. Each project began with the identification, surveillance, and capture of each new female. Those chosen had to have a certain set of criteria: a certain hair colour; they had to wear tight jeans, enjoy wearing high heels, look after their bodies; and, finally, they needed to really fancy him.

The several women that he'd had *relationships* with in the past had initially spurned his attention. They'd resisted his charm, even to the point of trying to throw him off their scent by calling him a weirdo, pervert, and sick bastard. But they were just playing hard to get. It was all part of the chase. As long as he pursued them for long enough, they would eventually fall for his charms and into his arms with only a little bit of a push on his part.

He fired up the browser on his laptop and opened up Facebook and Instagram. He punched away furiously on the keyboard, and within a few clicks, he found what he was looking for – his next project.

She was a corker. Hailey had been attractive, with her tall slender body, almond-shaped eyes, voluptuous lips and sultry looks. She had been an amazing find, but Rebecca outshone her. She knew how to pout and attract his attention. Her large breasts, hourglass figure and seductiveness had charmed him like no other had. That was why he hoped that Sally would let him keep Rebecca for a bit longer.

But his new project grabbed his attention for many reasons.

As he glanced through her profile pictures on Facebook, she was certainly plainer than Hailey and Rebecca. She dressed in tight jeans, heeled boots and tight tops, but there was something else about her that he found attractive. The nature of her character appealed to him as he played the secret video footage of her in Western Road.

He had stood behind her whilst she queued in several shops in town. It was her soft, kind demeanour that attracted him. She was delicate, almost to the point where if he'd shouted boo, she would jump out of her skin. The opportunity to explore her raw beauty proved too tempting an offer to let slip by.

On their many occasions together, Sally had told him that he needed to look beyond the exterior beauty of a person. She had stressed that his obsession with women was neither healthy nor attractive. He had vehemently argued in his defence, stating that he never intended to hurt anyone, but found that he couldn't help himself sometimes.

He knew there was another part of him that he couldn't

control. A part that got him into trouble on more than one occasion. As far back as he could remember, he had always had an infatuation with the female form.

He used to watch from a discreet distance as the girls from his year took part in netball practice at lunchtimes. Their tight white PE tops would stretch over their budding breasts.

He'd been too shy to ask anyone out. After all, he was just a nobody. He had been taunted for years by female classmates who gave him the nickname Pervy B after he was caught looking through the windows of the girls' changing rooms.

They never understood him. They never understood that he loved them; he admired and lusted over them.

He had enjoyed pinning Diane to the tree after school and forcing his hand inside her knickers. She had been walking home through the park and hadn't noticed him creep up on her. He hadn't known what all the fuss was about when he'd been expelled from school. After all, she had screamed her enjoyment and gripped his neck tight. She had loved it as much as he had; otherwise she wouldn't have been so vocal.

He knew even at that age that there were two halves to him.

The part that loved Diane, Hailey and Rebecca, and all the other girls and women he had discovered as projects was the part that now controlled him.

He unfolded the cotton bundle on his desk to reveal the cold shiny steel of the blade. The next project beckoned him as he switched off the light and headed into the dark night.

34

Scott had already been in a while before the rest of the team arrived. He'd spent the first hour of his shift briefing local officers. They had been tasked with conducting a search of the nineteen locations identified with marine engineering. He had set a radius of ten miles from Brighton, giving the officers a large area to scour. The search would extend as far as Newhaven in the east to Worthing in the west. With the multiple entry points and marinas along the coast, they would have their work cut out for them.

Their main task was to narrow down the potential locations and report back to Scott, who would then decide whether the shortlist required further investigation.

By mid-morning with the search well underway, nine of the nineteen locations had been ruled out as legitimate businesses.

Matt's email regarding the marine oil had given Scott and the team some hope and direction.

Scott had informed his boss about the decision to pull Helen off campus and leave the PCSO there to maintain the visible presence, much to Meadows's disapproval. It had led to a heated exchange in Meadows's office, with Scott arguing about the waste of valuable police resources leaving Helen on campus for too long.

Seeing DCI Berry head off in the direction of the press conference accompanied by Meadows filled Scott with a mixture of disappointment and anger. His exclusion sat uncomfortably with him.

With one eye on his phone, waiting for further updates from the local units, Scott joined the team gathered around the TV.

It was a welcome relief to see Helen stride back through the doors of the station. With the team stretched and multiple lines of enquiry, Scott needed every available officer in his team working on the cases.

"Good to have you back, Swifty," Mike announced as she walked in.

Abby beckoned them all to be quiet with a loud "Sssh."

Scott watched intently as the camera zoomed in on Meadows and DCI Berry sitting behind a desk draped in blue cloth. They both typically represented the professional, corporate image that Sussex Police liked to portray. They were both immaculately turned out. Meadows, in a dark grey suit, crisp white shirt and red tie, was matched by DCI Berry, who wore a dark grey two-piece skirt suit, white blouse, offset with a silver chain around her neck. Her dark brown hair shimmered under the lights and cameras that were trained on the pair.

In front of a sea of reporters, the pair gave formal introductions and the reasons for the press conference.

Meadows introduced DCI Berry as "An experienced senior officer drafted in specifically for this case due to her experience on similar cases, and was proving to be a valuable addition to the team."

When Meadows went on to say that the ongoing investigation had proved a challenge for the team, the team gave a collective gasp, not looking in Scott's direction.

Scott kept his anger firmly bottled up, while the team shook their heads in disbelief.

Meadows and Berry alternated as they released information to the press about the current cases and the unsolved cases in Essex. Meadows went on to appeal to members of the public to contact them if there was anything about these cases that they recognised. He also put out an extra request for any members of the public to get in touch who were in the area at the time of the abductions.

Pictures were shown of all the victims from both counties and the locations in which they were found, in the hope that it would jog some memories.

Meadows opened the floor to questions and was bombarded by reporters shouting in every direction. Mike tugged on Scott's sleeve and gave him a subtle nod to take a few steps back. The others continued to listen to the questions that were being thrown at both officers. Questions about links in forensics and why Essex Police were unable to identify any suspects. Why the unusual step of drafting in an Essex Police officer to oversee a Sussex case?

The questions faded into the background as Scott listened to what Mike had to say.

"Guv, listen, between you and me, DCI Berry has been asking me a lot of questions about you."

Scott quickly turned to look in Mike's direction; a look of concern creased the lines on his forehead.

"Like what?"

"Just loads of fishing questions, guv. Like how the team coped with Sian's death, whether it could have been preventable, what we think of you as a governor." Mike fell silent, raising his eyebrows to suggest that he didn't like her tone of questioning.

"I'm sure there's nothing in it, Mike," Scott said as he did his best to appear unfazed. In reality, his mind whirred around her ulterior motives.

"I didn't say much, guv. I just said and that with all due respect if she had questions about you, then she should ask you directly. I just made my excuses and said I needed to go for a piss." Mike shrugged. "Then she went and hit on Raj."

Scott took a deep breath before he slowly exhaled, in the hope that it would relax and calm his rising frustration.

"Thank you for telling me, Mike. I appreciate it."

Mike moved closer to Scott's ear.

"Off the record, guv, and between you and me, it feels like you're being done over. But I want you to know I've got your back."

35

Scott watched as Meadows and Berry had returned from the press conference. They had fielded a steady stream of questions from the gathered press corps, who had rapidly consumed details of the case as they were released during the conference. He thought the reporters from the *Argus* and BBC Sussex had been the most vocal with their questions. They had pushed Meadows to confirm whether the female students were safe to walk the streets at night.

Meadows had gone to great lengths to confirm that the police were using all available resources to ensure the safety of the female population on campus. Scott knew it wasn't an answer he was comfortable saying, but it had been the one that had been given to him by the Sussex Police press officer as a suitable response.

Watching on the TV screen alongside his team, Scott imagined how Meadows must have breathed a sigh of relief when a flurry of flashlights and rapid clicks of laptop keyboards concluded the press conference. Everyone was keen to write, edit, and upload their piece ahead of the pack.

It hadn't taken long for the press conference to have its desired effect. There had been a steady stream of phone calls to Scott's team. Whenever there was a press conference, their team usually fielded a mixture of relevant and irrelevant calls. As with any missing person enquiry, there were often several calls from worried family members whose loved ones had gone missing without a trace over the past months and years. Regardless, each call needed to be logged and evaluated. Many would lead the team up a blind alley.

Due to the nature of the cases involved, there were a higher-than-average number of calls from females concerned about their safety. Scott's team devoted a considerable amount of time to reassure them and give them advice on personal protection and safety.

The nature of several calls appeared promising. Two women had called to say that in recent weeks they had been approached by the driver of what appeared to be an unlicensed minicab. Neither of the women had accepted the offer of a lift, but both had given similar descriptions of the driver. He was a male, approximately aged thirty to forty years old, with small menacing eyes, a thin beard and flat cap, driving a blue Ford.

Scott paced around the incident board as he digested the descriptions. If anything, the descriptions seemed to suggest a disguise of some sort. He had lost count of the number of times suspects had used one to hide their real identity.

Nevertheless, this new information was added to the incident board, and local uniformed officers were sent to take more detailed statements from the women. If there was one certainty, every phone call needed to be evaluated for its importance. It would be nothing short of a catastrophe if they overlooked a call only to find that the information could have nailed a killer sooner.

The online portals for the local and national press organisations had been swift to broadcast the announcement:

FRENZIED ATTACKS ON LONE FEMALES BY SICK SERIAL KILLER.

The article hadn't gone down well with Scott or the press team. The press always had a way of creating sensationalised headlines to attract their readership.

First thing that morning and prior to the press briefing, Scott had instructed the Serious Crime Analysis Section to look into the links between the Essex and Sussex cases. SCAS was part of the National Crime Agency that dealt with organised and serious crime and investigated cases involving the potential emergence of serial killers and serial rapists at the earliest stage of their offending.

SCAS held a national database detailing serious sexual offences committed in the UK. Access to it would help Scott and the team to identify other similar cases across the country.

SCAS moved quickly and had already identified potential similarities with other cases over the past ten years that had been collated on ViCLAS, their Violent Crime Linkage Analysis System.

A quick email from SCAS confirmed the imminent arrival of the information that Scott had requested earlier.

The printer stirred into life. SCAS had called him to confirm that they were sending over their latest report.

"Come on, come on," he mumbled.

Why is it that when I want something urgently from the printer, it seems to sense my urgency and deliberately slows down?

He lifted the warm sheets of paper and thumbed through them, quickly scanning the main points. When there was a lull in the phone calls, Scott rallied the team together.

"Okay, team. SCAS has come through with some critical pieces of information. So far, they've identified three women in five years who have been murdered in exactly the same way, and a fourth potential victim. The first victim was a twenty-five-year-old female in Colchester. The second victim was a single mum of one, who was killed in Harlow. Finally, they also identified the case of a twenty-year-old female student in Paisley in Scotland who was stabbed, raped, and then killed in exactly the same way as Hailey Bratton."

"All redheads?" Helen asked.

Scott confirmed with a nod. "The fact that they were all redheads and our cases are all redheads gives us a new focus. SCAS are looking at known offenders who may have had a thing for that hair colour."

"That still doesn't give us much more to go on though, does it, guv?" Mike said.

"Well, yes and no. We know that someone's into redheads. We can cross-reference that against the sex offenders register, which SCAS is doing for us. We can look at any offenders who have served time for offences that carried the same MO. It also suggests that the offender has moved about. There is also one other potential victim that SCAS identified. There was a psychiatrist in Essex who went missing, presumed dead."

"Presumed?" Abby asked, raising a brow.

"The body was never found, but she was presumed to have died from her injuries. A cleaner at the practice discovered what she described as a bloodbath. There were signs of a violent struggle, but the victim was never found. Details of the report are coming over to us. As soon as it does, we need to look into it at once."

Scott wondered why DCI Berry hadn't mentioned any of these cases so far. Surely, she would have picked up on these cases during her cold case investigation?

36

She glanced at the small scrap of paper that had her scribbled shopping list on it. Rice pops, milk, a bag of apples, a small bunch of bananas and some loo roll.

With money tight, she would always hunt out the cheapest bargains, preferring instead to save her money for when she headed over to the union bar. A basket was all she needed as she hovered around the fruit aisle. A pack of six Royal Gala apples for one pound and ten pence would do nicely. She picked up a few packs and randomly turned them over, keen to find produce with the least amount of bruising.

It wasn't until she was walking around the fridge aisles that the hairs on the back of her neck stood on end. It sent a cold shiver down her spine.

She glanced over her shoulder, not sure why, but something made her feel uneasy. She saw nothing out of the ordinary. A mother was wheeling a trolley with an infant who happily chewed on a soggy biscuit. An older couple was discussing the merits of whether it was easier to carry two individual one-pint cartons or a single two-pint carton of milk. The only others she saw were two students.

She shook her head and carried on.

It wasn't until she stood near the toiletry products that she had that same feeling again. Earlier she had put that sensation down to being by the cold fridges. But now, she found herself feeling the same sensation.

She stopped mid-aisle and glanced over her shoulder again. Her eyes scanned the empty space. Nothing appeared odd. The usual sounds of a bustling supermarket bounced off the aisles around her, but nothing caught her attention. Yet something created an unease deep inside her, as if...

No, I'm just being stupid. It's just my imagination playing games with me.

As she went through the self-service checkouts, her mind raced. Her breath caught in her throat. Yet she couldn't explain the cold sweat or the heart palpitations.

Stop it; you're being stupid, she admonished herself as she took one last glance over her shoulder.

Outside, a Ford Focus raced past her, its horn tooting. She glanced around, unsure if someone was trying to get her attention.

The car pulled alongside and put on its hazard lights. The action made her jump; she let out a small scream and took a few steps back before laughing. She bent down to say something through the open passenger window.

She hadn't figured on her boyfriend picking her up.

37

The man threw the knife with such force that it rattled across the floor and bounced off the wall. The shrill, metallic sound echoed off the bare brick walls.

He hadn't planned on her boyfriend picking her up.

He walked around his desk, desperate to control his rapid breathing and the rage that boiled in his belly. He turned and slammed both fists on the table; the laptop and table lamp became airborne. His deep-throated scream tore through the silence.

"Bitch!" he yelled as he stared at the reflection of the man in the mirror. His eyes bulged, wide in anger, as he snarled, "Fucking bitch!"

He pounded the desk repeatedly.

He had come back empty-handed.

Failure wasn't in the plan.

He paced in circles. His mind spun like a vortex; his eyes darted from left to right as he searched for an explanation as to why his plan hadn't worked.

"Sally, I told you it was risky. These things need to be done on our terms. Look where it's got us?"

He pounded his left fist repeatedly as he sought answers from his own mind.

"Tell me, tell me, what do I do?"

His emotions flicked between flashes of calmness and anger.

"Think fast. I need to stay one step ahead of the police. Go back and get her? No, don't be stupid. That would be madness. It's too risky."

He paused mid-step and spun on his heel before racing over to the metal box. He unlocked the padlock and flipped open the lid.

Rebecca lay there, pale and semi-conscious. Her eyes flickered momentarily, a rasp escaping from her mouth. Shallow breaths vibrated in her chest, her mind and body shutting down.

"Rebecca, Rebecca. After everything I've done for you, you still prefer to sleep than engage with me in a civil conversation." He shook his head in disappointment. "I was hoping to bring you a gift. A playmate for you and me. But it didn't turn out the way I had hoped. Rebecca, are you listening to me?"

He gripped her arm and shook it a few times, trying to rouse her. Cold clamminess greeted his fingers, and he let go.

"You're not turning out to be the best project after all. I had high hopes for you. You were the best I'd ever come across," he said, glancing down at her naked form. "However, you've proved to be far too much trouble, and I'm not entirely sure how long you'll want to stay with us. I think it's time we parted company, don't you?"

With some effort, he dragged Rebecca out of the box and placed her gently on the floor. He undressed and lay beside her, stroking her soft, damp skin. He ran his fingers around the edges of one breast. Despite her worthlessness, he adored her body. She had curves in all the right places, just the way he liked it.

He pushed her hair to one side, leant in and whispered in her ear, "It's a pity you weren't more cooperative. We could have had lots of fun. Don't tell her, but I think Sally had a bit of a soft spot for you. I think she fancied you more than I did. You have to understand that there's only so much chasing I'm prepared to do. You kept sleeping and didn't really give us a chance to get to know you better."

She wouldn't be with them for much longer.

He sighed and pulled out a few sheets of bleach wipes, wanting her to look her best for her grand exit.

THIS TIME HE DROVE FARTHER. He had been tempted to drive back to the place where he had taken Hailey, but Sally had said it would probably attract too much attention.

Farther away from Shoreham is better.

He'd found the perfect location on Google Maps. A place void of disruption at this time of night.

As he gripped Rebecca around the waist and hauled her out of the boot, he noticed her lighter weight. Lighter than Hailey.

She whimpered in her semi-conscious state as her feet crashed to the ground. He dragged her through the hedges. Brambles and thorns snagged on his jeans, much to his annoyance. He held her firmly beneath her armpits as he dragged her through the dense shrub. The spot had been chosen carefully. It was nestled between the caravan campsite and the Scout campsite. He knew that the road might be slightly busier than the last location, but he had satisfied himself that he wouldn't be disturbed for the short period of time he would be there.

He laid Rebecca on her side, whilst he pulled out the ropes from his rucksack and found convenient spots from which to anchor them.

Having secured each arm to a length of rope, he strung her up between two trees. Her limp body collapsed to its knees. The force of the impact jolted Rebecca awake, her eyes rolling in their sockets for a brief moment before she closed them once again. She was too weak to fight or be fully aware of her dire situation. As shock made her pass out, he grimaced that her brief moment of pain had been so short lived. She drifted ever deeper into an unconscious state.

Using a small torch on the ground to illuminate the macabre scene, he stood back. He rested his hands on his hips and admired his handiwork. He expressed no emotion as he nodded once with satisfaction.

"Sometimes, these women make it far too easy for me. All I want to do is love them, and then they make me go and do this. Sally didn't want to come with me today to watch. She's waiting at home for me. I suspect she is getting the dinner on. Her speciality: beef bourguignon, with a nice glass of red to wash it down."

He circled Rebecca; her limp body hung like a wet towel on a washing line. Gravity pulled her body down and stretched the ropes taut.

"I was expecting you to put up more of a fight, but you've disappointed me. You've made it far too easy for me, too simple – a bit like you, really."

With a knife in one hand, he grabbed a fistful of Rebecca's hair with the other and pulled her head back. Her eyes barely opened with his face just inches from hers.

He pressed his lips to hers and kissed her tenderly. Her lips were cracked and dry, which annoyed him.

"Look at me when I'm talking to you," he demanded. When no response came, he changed tack. "Rebecca, sweetie, open your eyes. Show me that you love me."

Her eye muscles twitched for a fleeting moment. A wicked smile spread across his face. She'd just confirmed what he'd known all along. Rebecca loved him.

With the tip of his blade, he drew it across the side of her neck. She flinched as a trail of dark liquid erupted onto the skin's surface. Her life nectar was too precious to waste, so he leant in and gathered up the warm, sticky fluid on the tip of his tongue. His head spun, and he was briefly transported to a heavenly, giddy world.

She tasted sweet, dark and mystical.

The flesh wound opened up, releasing more of her lifeline, which drew him in even deeper.

Now in the final stages of his plan, he stepped back to admire his project.

Under darkness, the faint glow of the torch cast a ghostly hue on the scene. Rebecca, with her sweaty, dirty and matted hair, and her lifeless body, looked like an extra from a horror movie, or a rubber mannequin from the London Dungeons.

He had no need for her now. He'd proved once again that he could have any woman he wanted. Sally would be proud of him.

As he knelt down in front of her, he ran his finger across her navel before following the same path with his steel blade. Rebecca's skin tore with little resistance, and the knife burrowed deep from one edge to the other. Her body spewed blood and fluid. With no barrier holding them back, her intestines plopped out of her abdominal cavity.

He looked down in delight as the tangled mess of her innards pooled between her knees. The soft, slippery organ felt wet and slimy between his fingers like a thin balloon filled with water.

His work was done. Rebecca could rest now.

Her innards will prove a hearty meal for the nocturnal creatures.

38

A rare evening off gave Scott the chance to spend quality time with Cara. Guilt never seemed that far from Scott's mind when a job consumed him mentally and physically.

But Cara understood in spite of her disappointment over Scott's recent absence, which made their evening out just that more special.

They'd driven over to the marina and spent the evening relaxing over a few glasses of wine as the sun made its journey down. The golden sunset offered the perfect setting as they sat hand in hand, saying very little. They soaked up the vibe and buzz of a warm summer's evening.

Scott felt the stress drain from his body as his tight shoulders began to loosen and drop. "You okay, babes?"

Cara squeezed his hand. "I couldn't be happier at this precise moment." She looked at him from behind her brown shades. "You do know that I miss you all the time, don't you? I know we're both really busy with work, and unfortunately, that can make our lives a little unpredictable. That doesn't stop you from occupying my thoughts."

Scott nodded and squeezed her hand in return. Cara had a lovely way with her words and always made him feel so wanted and needed. He only hoped that he made her feel the same in return. No matter how bad his week had been, just knowing that he'd be seeing Cara made it worth it.

They walked slowly around the marina, their bodies firmly connected after Scott threw an arm around Cara and pulled her close. They paused by the menu boards of several restaurants, deciding where to have a meal. They finally settled on Bella Italia, grabbed a seat by the window, and ordered ribs for Scott and grilled chicken for Cara.

Scott looked off into the distance.

"Scottie, are you okay? You just seem a little distant," Cara asked.

He smiled and leant over the table to give Cara a soft kiss. "I'm so sorry, babes. It's been a crazy time at work, and I guess I'm just finding it hard to switch off."

"Promise?"

"Yes, of course."

"Am I boring you with my crap?"

Scott laughed and said, "No, not at all."

Cara gave him a mock stern look. "Okay, but you look stressed. Is work getting to you? Your new DCI on your case?"

"You could say that. Meadows thinks the sun shines out of Berry's arse. The saviour who's going to restore credibility to CID."

"Is she that good?"

Scott paused before answering, "She's another political player like Meadows. She *needs* to be seen taking charge."

"Is she ruffling feathers in your team? You worried about it?"

"A bit, but nothing I can't handle," he replied, keen to gloss over DCI Berry's involvement in the case. "Besides, tonight isn't about work. It's about us. I don't want anything spoiling this evening, and to be honest, I could really do with..." He smiled wickedly.

Cara smirked. "All good things come to those who wait, and I promise you, I'm worth the wait."

"So is my luck in, then?"

"You know your luck is always in, Scott Baker."

SCOTT SNUGGLED into Cara's comforting, naked warmth. He smiled sleepily as his knees 'docked' perfectly with hers.

"Morning, sleepyhead," he whispered.

Cara pulled his outer thigh closer to her. She made the slightest of "Mmms" in agreement.

The summer sun broke through the curtains, breaking up the darkness and heralding a new day.

Scott groaned and slipped out of bed. He stood for a moment and stretched his arms out to shake off the sleepiness. "Coffee and your yucky Special K?"

"Mmm, yes, please. Lots of it, because I'm starving," she said, her voice muffled from beneath the duvet.

"I'm not surprised after last night."

"Are you complaining?" Cara said as her head emerged from under the covers. She rolled over into the warm space vacated by Scott and pulled his pillow deep into her face.

"I can smell you."

Scott laughed and headed downstairs to the kitchen. Within a few minutes he returned, a tray between both hands. "Your breakfast is served, madam."

Cara sat up in bed and tucked the duvet around her sides. She sipped eagerly from her mug as she watched Scott rummage in his wardrobe for something to wear. He held a dark blue tie against his navy suit and debated the merits of whether the two coordinated.

"You could have stuck a rose between your butt cheeks like in *Cold Feet*," she teased as she glanced at his naked backside.

"I'm getting too old for this," he said on a lazy yawn.

"What – too old for sex or too old to handle me?"

Scott glanced at her and cracked a smile. "I meant getting up for work so early. Besides, I think I can handle you – just about. I don't see you complaining. And don't you dare say anything to Abby; I know how thick you two are."

Cara beckoned him over and put her bowl to one side.

"You more than satisfy me, and you certainly know your way around the female form. Thank you, that was perfect, and breakfast wasn't bad either." She laughed before giving Scott a long, lingering kiss.

Cara threw off the duvet and lay there warm and naked. "Now how about you show me once again just how *much* you fancy me."

39

Buoyed up with the Cara feel-good factor, Scott was in a good mood. A night out with Cara had been the perfect remedy to his stress. An opportunity to leave the job behind and feel normal for a few hours. His mind cast back to how they had mingled with the crowd, just another couple enjoying each other's company for an evening.

His evening might have gone to plan, but the case was slowly skidding sideways, and he didn't have his foot on the brake. He stared at the incident board while slapping a ruler into one palm. The pictures of Hailey Bratton and Rebecca Thorne smiled back at him. He cast an eye over their youthful features, exuberance, and the freshness radiating from their faces. Pleasant thoughts of them were soon cast to one side when he looked at the SOCO evidence and post-mortem pictures of Hailey Bratton.

The system files had been updated with progress on the searches being conducted on the marine engineering units. So far, the searches had yielded nothing. It wasn't the news he had hoped for, which soured his mood further. New instructions had been passed to the search team to extend the search to former businesses and as far back as ten years.

The gaps of information on the incident board played on his mind. Everyone was working flat out, but frustration tinged his positive thoughts. The job, dwindling budgets, limited resources, and constant management reports about crime figures threw up a series of hurdles that modern-day senior police officers had to navigate.

Abby came into the office, dumped her bag by the side of her desk, and placed a large one-litre bottle of mineral water by her PC.

"That might be regarded as an offensive weapon!" she shouted across the floor.

Scott looked at her in confusion. When Abby nodded at the ruler in his hand, he laughed.

"Time for some brekkie?" Abby asked.

"Normally it's me who's suggesting breakfast...or lunch – or come to think of it, just food in general."

"I know, but it was a manic rush this morning. I couldn't get the kids up. I just about managed to get myself out on time. And now I'm starving."

SCOTT TUCKED into smoked salmon and scrambled eggs on toast. On this occasion, Abby stole the show as she heartily tucked into a full English breakfast, much to Scott's amusement.

Abby was the kind of person who would often forget to eat. A combination of a hectic work life and a busy home life often meant that she had neither the time nor the inclination to prepare something for herself. Scott had pulled her up on many an occasion for having a bowl of cereal for dinner the night before. He'd lectured her on missing vital nourishment for her body. It often fell on deaf ears, and Abby would shrug it off.

"How're things with Jonathon?" Scott asked, waiting for Abby to finish her mouthful.

"Touch wood," she replied, tapping her head, "It's actually going really well. In fact, it's almost going too well."

"You sound surprised, as if you were expecting it to fall at the first hurdle?"

Abby shrugged and said, "Well, you know what I'm like. I make bad choices when it comes to men. I'm a difficult person to get on with, and I like things done in a certain way. I thought he would leg it at the first opportunity."

"So has he restored your faith in men?"

Abby blushed, offering nothing more than a sheepish grin and a shrug of her shoulders.

"Oh, I get it. The jury is still out?"

"No! I just...like this relationship. He's kind, thoughtful and really laid-back, which I actually think is good for me. He helps to balance me and my life. Up until this point, my life felt like one long rollercoaster ride. Bad luck and poor judgement have shafted me on more than one occasion, and if I'm honest, it's left me with a negative and critical perspective of life and relationships."

"That's really cheered me up," Scott teased. "I'm glad we came out for breakfast now."

"Sorry, sorry. I didn't mean to go on. You know what I'm like when I get on my soapbox."

"It's cool. Don't worry. I'm just glad that you're happy for a change."

"Well, I've told Jonathon about you and Cara. And..." Abby paused before continuing, "I suggested to Jonathon that maybe we could go out as a foursome for a bite to eat one evening. I was a bit apprehensive as to what he might say, but he seemed really enthusiastic about the whole thing. He's heard loads about you, and I actually think he's quite fascinated by what Cara does."

"Blimey, that must be serious if you're thinking of meals and foursomes."

"Oh, he's a really nice fella. He helped out last night, as it was Adam's birthday. I took Adam and five friends to the Hollywood Bowl, and Jonathon came and helped out."

Scott's eyes widened. "You're kidding? We were there last night at the marina for a few drinks and a meal."

Abby threw her hands up in the air in mock despair. "Now you tell me. You could have come and rescued me from six screaming boys. Any civilised company would have been a godsend."

"Ah, yes, but you had Jonathon with you. Are you saying that he's not civilised company?"

Abby cracked a smile. "I meant I could have left him with the kids and escaped."

"Yes, and I think you'd have never seen him after that," Scott replied.

40

Scott sat in his chair and scooted closer to the desk. He felt cheerful this morning. In fact, he couldn't remember the last time a morning had gone so well.

He thought back to Cara lying naked in his bed, then the good catch-up with Abby. Cara was a good influence on him. Yes, they had their ups and downs, but it had been a few years since he'd felt this happy. But Tina and Becky were never far from his thoughts. His heart squeezed when he remembered Becky smiling and screaming 'Daddy' each time he came in from work. Work hassles would melt away on seeing her face light up.

Scott opened his phone and flicked through the gallery of pictures until he found one of Becky.

A knock on the open door of his office jolted him out of his melancholic moment.

Berry was leaning up against the door frame, one arm folded across her chest, the other playing with the necklace pendant around her neck.

Is she stalking me now?

Every time he turned his head, she was there. If someone

had it in for him up there, then they were doing a bloody good job of letting him know.

"Yes, ma'am?" Scott hated the need to formally address her. The words almost stuck in his throat. He fiddled with his phone.

Berry stepped into the room and closed the door. The edges of her mouth curved into the smallest of smiles as her dark brown eyes locked on him. She helped herself to one of the seats opposite Scott, who was now feeling more uncomfortable.

"I've been thinking, Scott. Why don't we mix business with pleasure?" she asked, raising an eyebrow suggestively. "It would just be like old times again."

Scott shook his head as he stared at her.

Berry added, "If I recall correctly, I don't remember you complaining in the past..."

There was an uncomfortable silence as she waited for an answer from Scott. Thick tension filled the space between them.

"With all due respect, ma'am, I'm not interested. Nor do I think it's an appropriate suggestion on your part as a senior officer."

"Scott, I don't think you're getting the message," she said, her voice laced with firm brevity he'd not yet heard from her since her arrival. He'd clearly annoyed her with his dismissal. "You wouldn't want Meadows hearing that you've been uncooperative with me, or that you withheld information from me, would you? From what I can tell, you're already on thin ice."

The clinical coldness of Berry's tone and threat both stunned and angered Scott. His body tensed with ire, his stomach churned, and it took every ounce of resolve to suppress a reaction. He crossed his arms and simply glared at her.

Berry turned the screw as she said, "Your current thing, Cara, she's very beautiful. You still have a soft spot for brunettes, then?"

When Scott didn't respond, she continued, "Is she really doing it for you like I used to? I think it would be nice to have a chat over a drink, just like old times. You never know where it might lead?" she said, a glint in her eye.

"Thanks but no thanks. I think we've moved on from that. If you haven't, then that's your problem, but I know I have. And for the record, yes, Cara is a beautiful, lovely and amazing woman."

Scott kept his voice even as he emphasised his point. Deep within, he seethed. Over the past few months, everything that he had taken years to build was slowly being eroded.

He stood from his chair and splayed his hands on his desk.

Whether it was perfect timing or not, Abby knocked on the door and let herself in. She exchanged glances with Scott and Berry.

"Is everything okay, ma'am? Guv?" Abby said.

Berry stood from her seat and straightened her jacket. She took a few steps towards Abby and offered her a melodramatic smile. "Everything is fine, Abby. Just a couple of officers disagreeing over something."

Abby turned to watch Berry stroll casually out of the office and out of earshot. She faced Scott and held out her hands, searching for an answer.

Scott closed his eyes and shook his head. "Don't. Whatever you do, just don't."

Abby rolled her eyes. "Guv, get your jacket and come with me. No argument about it."

Scott and Abby cut through from Edward Street and St James's Street out on to Marine Parade in silence before they came upon an empty bench.

"Off the record, and as a friend, what was all that about? I could hear it kicking off from outside, and before anyone else heard it, I had to butt in."

Scott stared ahead, his mind a whirlwind of emotions.

He shook his head, feeling his body heave with sadness.

He exhaled heavily and said, "It doesn't matter, Abby, seriously. I just have a habit of attracting shit into my life, and once it's there, it never goes away."

"Listen, whatever it is, we can get through this. I promise you. Have I ever let you down?"

Scott shook his head again, unwilling to open his eyes and face reality or, more to the point, face Abby.

"Please. I hate seeing you like this. Listen, I'll only say this once because I don't want your ego getting any bigger, but you're my best friend, and I care about you. I really do."

Scott opened his eyes and stared ahead. "I've got a history with Berry."

"History? As in you've had a run-in with her before?"

Scott blew out a breath and turned to Abby. "No, I mean *history*."

It took a few moments for Abby to understand what Scott really meant. "History? Oh...as in *that* type of history."

Scott nodded.

"Oh, shit."

"Exactly."

Abby said nothing, clearly waiting for Scott to elaborate.

Scott stared at the ground. "I really screwed up. I was young, naïve and, dare I say, impressionable. Berry...she was a predator. Still is. She enjoyed male attention, and between you and me and the gatepost, she was the cause of the breakup of at least two marriages. Everyone knew she dated senior officers, and that's why she's where she is now. I think she deliberately did it to advance her career. She got rapid promotion and secondments to special projects and task forces. The woman has no scruples."

Abby nodded in bewilderment; her eyes were fixed wide as she tried to process Scott's admission.

"So, if she dated senior officers, no disrespect, why did she come after you?"

"Because I guess I was young and keen. To be honest, I don't really know. She charmed me. She was seriously attractive. We first started chatting one night in a pub. Too much booze, I guess. She hinted at the possibility of putting in a good word for me when it came to promotions. Then we seemed to bump into each other on nights out. On one particular occasion, one drink led to another and another... and well, I don't need to paint you a picture. It turned into a regular thing for a while."

Scott looked at Abby, feeling embarrassed. "What a mess. I hoped – in fact, I prayed that this would stay in my past."

"So why is she here? Is her assignment really case related?"

Scott shrugged. "Probably not. Things between us ended on a sour note. She started seeing a DI from another nick about the same time as me. He was as bent as a nine-bob note. Mixed with local criminality. The kind you'd find at Raquels in Basildon, or the Epping Forest Country Club on a Friday or Saturday night. Some nasty pieces of work who wouldn't hesitate in pulling out a 'shorty' and giving you both barrels. I'd seen him hand her an envelope one night before she came to mine. Whilst she was asleep, I... Well, I checked the envelope in her bag. Five grand in cash!"

Abby gasped. "Did you confront her?"

"I did, and said I'd have to report what I'd witnessed and discovered. She laughed it off. Told me to stop being a goody two shoes. By then my prints were already on the envelope. It was my word against hers and the DI she met. I was so wet behind the ears that I didn't think anyone would believe the word of a junior officer against two senior officers."

Scott sighed. "To make matters worse, it wasn't till much later that I found out she'd recorded our conversation on her phone and doctored the recording to make it sound like I'd received the five grand and she'd found it on me. So it was either keep my mouth shut or get kicked out."

"That's blackmail! So do you reckon she's here to stir up trouble?"

"Your guess is as good as mine, Abby. She could be here because of her cold cases, but we could have shared this information online. Any one of the cold case officers could have contacted us. Why she made a direct approach to Sussex is what worries me."

Abby shook her head in disbelief. She reached into her pocket and pulled out her phone, which was vibrating with an incoming message.

"Well, we'll have to talk about this later. Looks like we've got more pressing issues," she said as she showed Scott her phone screen.

41

It felt like déjà vu for Scott as he made his way with Abby along the A27 Shoreham bypass. It had only been a matter of days since they had last visited the area upon the discovery of Hailey Bratton's body.

Reports had come in detailing the discovery of another female body, believed to be Rebecca Thorne, not far off the A27. That in itself was a vital piece of the jigsaw as far as Scott was concerned. The remote location of both bodies suggested that the killer had a detailed knowledge of the area, and this could assist Scott in narrowing down the geographical area for their search.

Coombes Road was an isolated single-track road that spurred off north from the A27 and ran parallel to the River Adur. With tall trees and shrubs that lined the road either side, it provided a natural camouflage from prying eyes.

As he made his way along the track, many sections fell into darkness where the trees formed a canopy above the road. Those dense sections sporadically opened up into small hedgerows that formed a natural boundary to the ploughed fields beyond. He drove past a gated driveway with an iron gate on the left, which had the Scout Association symbol pinned to it. Scott made a mental note to check to see whether any Scout troops had been camping there last night. Door-to-door enquiries appeared out of the question, as Scott had yet to see any properties along this stretch of the road.

He pulled up behind the familiar sight of random emergency vehicles. Scott could see a handful of police cars, a scientific services van, Matt Allan's car and Cara's silver Ford Focus. A black private ambulance had parked up, ready to take the body away when forensics had finished their work.

As he and Abby walked towards the blue and white outer cordon, Scott stopped and sighed heavily as he looked off into the distance. Abby followed his line of sight until she saw DCI Berry deep behind the police cordon, instructing several SOCOs as they went about their work.

"Don't let her get to you," Abby said. "Stay calm, keep your chin up, and let's catch this killer before she does."

PC Willits as scene guard was in charge of the log. Abby and Scott signed in with her. She gave both Scott and Abby a respectful nod before handing them the usual disposable pack containing a suit, covers for their shoes, gloves and a paper mask.

Scott studied the landscape. Officers swarmed around in different directions outside of the cordon. Within the blue and white taped zone peacefulness reigned as silent figures went about their work. The location bore striking similarities to the location where they'd found Hailey's body. A quiet single-track road and dense foliage lined both sides of the road, offering limited visibility to the area. Everything about the killer's modus operandi seemed well planned and, sadly, well executed.

Raj and Helen were already on scene and busy taking notes as they liaised with Matt. Cara had completed her preliminary investigation and was writing up her notes and recording evidence into her Dictaphone app.

It was Scott's worst fears. The lifeless, pale body of Rebecca Thorne hung between two trees as the forensics officers conducted a detailed grid search of the ground surrounding her. Photos had been taken of her in position, and Cara had been given the opportunity to examine her closely.

With her head hung low, Scott couldn't see Rebecca's face, which was probably a blessing. Her entrails were scattered around her in a wide arc of at least twelve feet. Despite how close he was to the body, the organs were indistinguishable, looking like random pieces of anatomy that had been torn, ripped, and discarded. The scene created a vivid picture in Scott's mind of the horrific acts that must have been inflicted on her before her death. Small red wounds littered her lower limbs where the flesh had been torn from her body.

Scott dropped his head briefly as a mark of respect for the loss of yet another young life with a bright future.

Cara joined him. "It's pretty much the same as the last one. A small cut to her neck and what appears to be smear marks, and obviously the large incision to her abdomen. The cause of death was excessive blood loss. There's generalised skin irritation over at least sixty per cent of her body. It looks similar to Hailey's, so I'm guessing it's some type of ammonia-based substance again. This poor girl really suffered. The way her organs have been scattered over the scene suggests that foxes, rats and suchlike are responsible for the mess. The bite marks to her lower limbs would substantiate that theory. Lividity is present, so she's been here for at least six to twelve hours." Cara added, "I've got one post-mortem to do this afternoon, so I'll get this started as soon as we have a confirmed ID."

Scott was lost for words. The savagery of the attack horrified him. To be strung up was barbaric in itself, but to be disembowelled as well. He shook his head in disbelief.

What kind of demented psycho would do this?

"Your missing student?" Cara asked.

"From the looks of it, I'd say she fits the description. Female, pale complexion, red hair, trim figure..." He trailed off as his gaze returned to the body.

"Scott, good of you to finally turn up!" Berry shouted as she walked in his direction. "I've got everything under control; I couldn't wait for you to get here. I've sent uniform to do some legwork. There's a farm, Coombes Farm, up the road, and a Scout camp back in the direction that we came from. I've got some local boys conducting enquiries."

Scott was both uncomfortable and annoyed by Berry's tone and her commandeering the scene even though it wasn't on her patch. He was just about to formally introduce Cara as Dr Hall, but Berry waved him off.

"No need, we've already met." Berry looked and Cara. "Dr Hall, I look forward to the outcome of your post-mortem. As you can imagine, this case is a pressing priority for myself and the team."

Cara offered nothing more than a nod.

"And I also want to say, Dr Hall, that Scott has been incredibly helpful and very *generous* with his time and attention. He has gone to great lengths to welcome me. I don't know if you're aware, but he's stayed back on several evenings just to help me."

Scott shot Berry a stern glance, seething fury at her loaded innuendos and suggestive comments. Her smug smile hinted that she revelled in the moment and enjoyed seeing him squirm. He needed to bide his time. She was backing herself into a corner and didn't know it.

Berry added, "I'll head back now that I've wrapped up here. I'll leave you to oversee the scene, Scott."

She strode off purposefully, barking a few final orders at the assembled officers as she went. "Make yourselves useful and stop wasting time."

Scott and Cara were joined by Matt and Abby as they stood in a moment's silence in the aftermath of Berry's whirlwind.

"Thanks for the warning, mate," Matt said sarcastically. "She doesn't mince her words, does she?"

"Sorry, Matt, I didn't know she was here until I got here myself. Has she ruffled a few feathers?"

Matt pursed his lips. "My officers didn't take too kindly to her throwing her weight around. I think they know how to do their job, don't you?"

"Will you apologise on my behalf, mate?" Scott said. "Diplomacy isn't her strength, especially when it comes to lower-ranking officers and civvies."

"You're telling me," Matt replied as he headed back to his team. "Keep her off our backs if you can, Scott."

"Another satisfied customer?" Abby said.

Scott ignored her. His emotions over Berry were clouding his judgement over the cases, and that didn't sit well with him.

"Hello?"

Scott blinked and looked at Abby. "Sorry, I was just thinking."

She rolled her eyes as she stuffed her phone back in her pocket. "Listen, ignore the black widow. I've got better news. Even though we've pretty much ruled him out because of his age and the Essex cases, Freddie Coltrane has been picked up on campus in relation to the evidence we found on his camera. Raj called also to say that Mistress Claire called earlier with some telling information. I'll fill you in on the way to the station."

42

Freddie Coltrane slouched in his chair, looking thoroughly bored. With arms folded and his legs fully extended beneath the table, he stared ahead.

Scott wasn't surprised to find that upon their arrival at the station, Freddie's solicitor had only arrived within minutes of Freddie being taken into custody. Scott imagined that Freddie's father had arranged for Beecham, a London solicitor, to deal with the ongoing investigations into Freddie. Beecham probably had pound signs in his eyes.

Sitting opposite the pair in the interview room, Scott noticed Beecham's impatience as he glanced at his watch every few minutes. Damn selfish lawyers and their billable hours.

"How are you, Freddie?" Scott asked.

Freddie shrugged and continued his nonchalant attitude.

"Where have you been the last few days, Freddie? I assume you know now that we searched your room in halls?"

"No comment."

Beecham interrupted, "On what grounds did you decide

to use force to enter my client's room?" His voice was stern and abrupt, like most solicitors.

"For your information, Mr Beecham, we had no reason to use force because the door was open."

Beecham shot Freddie a look to express his dissatisfaction.

"We found some interesting items in a shoebox," Scott began as Abby slid some clear plastic evidence bags across the table. "Item number one, a pair of women's knickers. We've identified them as belonging to Hailey Bratton. Item number two, another pair of women's knickers. We've identified that they belong to Lucy Wheeler."

Whilst delivering the forensic feedback, Scott watched for visible changes in Freddie's behaviour, through either his facial or body movements.

"Item number three is another pair of women's knickers, which we will come back to in a moment." Scott tapped item number four for emphasis. "Here you will see printouts of pictures and videos that we found on the memory card inside a Nikon D3200 DSLR camera. Incidentally, your prints were found on the camera and the memory card within it. They contain images and recordings of an unknown male committing a series of violent sexual assaults on several women, again identities unknown. Each victim asks the male to stop, but he continues to assault them. Do you know anything about this?"

Freddie lifted his eyes to Scott before saying, "No...comment."

"Are any of the women in the stills Hailey Bratton, Rebecca Thorne, or...Yana Melnik?"

Abby scratched down notes as the interview continued.

Scott noticed a tiny muscular twitch above Freddie's left eye when he mentioned Yana Melnik's name.

"Were you present during the filming of these assaults?"

"No comment."

"Freddie, I put it to you that you were the male in these videos who committed these acts. And we have a victim statement from Yana claiming you sexually assaulted her on several occasions against her will."

"My client's not at liberty to answer that question," Beecham said.

Freddie gave a wry smile.

Scott tapped on evidence bag number three once again. "Item number three is yet again another pair of female knickers. They belong to Mistress Claire."

A rapid flicker of his eyes was the first sign of Freddie's nerves.

Scott continued, "You see, we know that you were very angry, and that you wanted Mistress Claire to hurt you because you had been bad. What did you do that was so bad?"

"No comment."

Scott waited a few moments. He'd found that silent moments during the interview often unnerved a suspect. The person would inevitably say something to fill the silence. But on this occasion, Freddie continued to remain deceptively cool.

Scott said, "Were you referring to the fact that you had harmed and sexually assaulted Yana and perhaps other females such as Hailey or Rebecca?"

Beecham interrupted again. "My client is not at liberty to answer that question. Unless you have evidence, such an accusation is purely subjective."

Scott waved Yana's victim statement in Beecham's face. "It took some reassurance on our part that no harm would come to her, but here's your evidence."

Scott rested his elbows on the table. He glared at Freddie. "Freddie, I know you like Mistress Claire to hurt you and do all those other things that your little twisted mind gets a kick from. Did you then perform these acts on other women?"

Beecham said, "Inspector, these are nothing but spurious claims that are unsubstantiated. I strongly protest you coercing my client into admitting to something that he has no knowledge of. I ask that you refrain from this line and style of questioning and either terminate this interview or charge my client."

Scott nodded slowly without averting his gaze from Freddie. "You see, Freddie, I'm going to find out who those women are in those videos. I hope for your sake that you're not the person committing those indecent sexual assaults. Because if that's you, then no fancy lawyer's going to be able to protect you." Scott glanced at Beecham as he delivered the final few words. "If you think you're safe, I'd reconsider. I'd really be worried if I were you."

FRUSTRATION STILL ATE at Scott as he sat at his desk, pondering the outcome of Freddie's interview. His gut feeling told him that Freddie was unlikely to be a murderer, but without a doubt he was the person in the videos. Freddie was proving to be more of a slippery character than Scott had anticipated.

With his phone in one hand, he tapped the tip of his pen on the desk in a slow rhythmic fashion as he thought about Freddie and his potential connection with the victims. His thoughts were interrupted when Berry knocked on his door and walked in without giving Scott an opportunity to respond.

"Ma'am, with all due respect, I get the impression that there's more to your transfer to our team than meets the eye."

She smiled coyly. "There's no hidden agenda, Scott. I

believe we're after the same killer, so it made sense for us to pool our resources and knowledge. But..." She paused for a few moments as she stared intently in Scott's direction. "Since I got here, it's stirred up the past between us, and I've not stopped thinking about you."

"That may be, ma'am, but that was then. This is now. And I'm not interested. As I said before, I don't think it's appropriate."

"Scott, you're certainly more forceful than I remember. But I think you'll see it my way. You have your career to think of...and your relationship. Besides, I like it here; a change of scenery might do me the world of good." She dropped a small scrap of paper on Scott's desk. "This is where I'm staying whilst in Brighton. I'm free this evening, so I'll expect you later. Don't let me down, Scott."

Scott sat back in his seat, stunned into silence. He dropped his phone. She had breezed in and then breezed out. In that brief sixty seconds in between, she had once again turned his world upside down. He rested his head in the palms of his hands, void of all emotions. A dark emptiness, a black vortex spiralled inside him, raining confusion down on him from all angles.

He felt trapped in the same way he had all those years ago. No one would believe him, certainly not Meadows. Scott already knew that Meadows loved her. Berry was everything that DCI Harvey wasn't. Dynamic, aggressive, charming. A good manager. Meadows had been impressed by how she always seemed to pull the best out of her teams in Essex. He might not have agreed with all of her tactics, but she had been judged on her results, and they spoke volumes.

As Scott sat there contemplating his situation, he recalled Meadows saying in a previous conversation that "Berry would be a good catch for us and a valuable asset to the division long-term." That conversation had rung alarm bells for Scott. It now felt like the nightmare of Berry would never go away.

His mind drifted to Cara, beautiful Cara. He needed her more than anything else, and the worry of losing her seeped in bone-deep as he was getting pulled into the pit of Berry's endless games. Cara kept him grounded, had supported him during his dark moments, and had helped him come to terms with the loss of his family. It was Cara whom he looked forward to seeing every day. He needed to tell her everything.

He felt like he was getting hit from all angles and had nowhere to turn and no one to help him. He began to dial Abby's number but was interrupted by the ring of his internal phone.

He picked up and smiled at Raj's news.

The breakthrough he needed was about to hit him full on.

43

Scott raced to the incident board as the team huddled around to watch Raj pin up crucial information that had been received.

"What have we got, Raj?" he asked, excitement in his voice.

"Guv, SCAS came back with further information about the psychiatrist victim in Essex. Her case goes back five years. She was a *redhead*, and her name was Sally Martin. She'd been in private practice as a psychiatrist for more than fifteen years and before that, for seven years in the NHS. She lived in Manningtree, Essex, but worked in the outskirts of Colchester. She specialised in treating people with extreme and violent psychiatric issues. She seemed well respected in her field. Sally had produced numerous online articles in her areas of expertise."

Raj paused for a moment as he checked his notes. "From initial findings, she produced written pieces on issues such as psychological and psychosocial interventions for negative symptoms in psychosis. She's written stuff about cortisol as a predictor of psychological therapy response in depressive disorders, and finally, about diffusion tensor imaging predictors of treatment outcomes in major depressive disorder. And that's just three of over fifty articles. But I haven't got a clue what any of those articles are referring to." He shrugged in confusion.

"Excellent, at least we have a name and more background," Scott said.

Berry entered through the swing doors and strode towards the team with purpose. Those gathered paused to look over. She waved off the distraction and indicated for Raj to continue.

"And a picture, guv," Raj said, pinning up a picture of a smart-looking female with a thin face and shiny red hair tied up in a ponytail. With a cream blouse and two-piece grey suit, she looked the consummate medical professional.

A silence fell over the team as they stared at the image.

Raj once again looked to enjoy being the focal point of those gathered. "They've pulled off a bit more, guv. Police records indicate that she lodged a harassment case against a patient about five years ago. Those details should be coming through to us at some point. Obviously, we don't actually know what happened to her, and there's no evidence to confirm her death. But this might be interesting: Sally Martin also had nineteen thousand pounds cleared out of her bank just after her disappearance."

"Listen, team, we don't want to wait for any records to come to us." There was a new urgency in Scott's tone as he paced in front of the incident board. "Get onto it now; chase up all the records. Anything you can find on this patient. Go straight to the top of the trust if you have to. We also need to speak to Sally's friends, family and any business colleagues. Dig up anything you can. It could be a wild goose chase, but my gut instinct suggests otherwise."

Scott paused for a moment whilst he gathered his

thoughts. He only had one chance to get this right, so needed to make sure he had his sequence of thoughts in the right order.

"Check prison records as well. Look for anyone who was recently released after a five-year stretch. Speak to the integrated offenders' management team as well just to tie up loose ends. Get local officers from Essex involved if necessary to do some of the legwork for you." Scott glanced at Berry, who reluctantly nodded. "Any aggravation from Essex, refer them directly to DCI Berry."

Scott left Mike, Raj, and Helen in a flurry of activity as they busily hit their phones. This new angle brought with it fresh optimism.

Scott and Abby's next appointment was at the post-mortem of the victim they had found that morning. Rebecca's father had sadly confirmed the victim as being his daughter just moments earlier after the FLO, more commonly known as a family liaison officer, had sent Scott a text confirmation.

They were just about to leave when DCI Berry invited herself along, much to Scott's annoyance. After the exchange they'd had earlier, the prospect of being in the same room as Abby, Cara and DCI Berry filled him with a gut-wrenching dread.

The only thought on his mind was whether Berry was going to drop any more innuendos in front of Cara.

44

There was an awkward silence in the car as Scott drove Abby and Berry to the mortuary. To her credit, Abby tried to offer passing comments to break the silence, but the conversation stayed muted at best. Scott occasionally glanced in his rear-view mirror and caught a glimpse of Berry staring back without expression. At times, it felt like she was fixated on the back of his head as he drove, a feeling that made the hairs on his neck prickle.

After being let in by one of the mortuary technicians, the trio were shown to an area where they threw on some protective robes. Berry opted to view the post-mortem from the raised inspection area. The bitter combination of decaying bodies, bodily fluids, and disinfectant hung in the air and assaulted their nostrils. Of the three, a grimacing Abby appeared to find it hardest to put up with the smell.

The cadaver was laid out on the table, with the examination of her body already advanced. With the preliminaries like her weight and height already recorded, Cara was now onto her examination of the victim's neck region, where she was taking swabs.

"Thanks for scheduling this PM so quickly, Cara. What have you got so far?" Scott asked.

Cara paused and stood back in the way a sculptor would admire their work. "With regards to this lady, she has hypostatic discolouration from both knees downwards. This would suggest her final resting position was the one we found her in and the position she was killed in. I'd also say that she's been dead for between twelve and eighteen hours. I can't be more precise than that without knowing what the temperature was outdoors last night, and what her body temperature was when she was taken to the scene."

The officers nodded.

"She also has discolouration through extensive bruising around the upper abdomen, armpits and chest regions."

"From?" Scott asked.

"My guess would be that these types of mark are consistent with what you might get if the victim was dragged in a bear-hug type of hold."

Scott took in each piece of detail as he built a mental picture of the final moments of the victim's life. However, he found it hard to concentrate during the visit. His mind and attention flicked to Berry, who stood motionless with her arms folded as she stared down at the scene from the raised area.

"Can you tell me anything about the knife wound?" Scott was keen to hurry up this discussion and leave the claustrophobic environment that felt like a vice grip around his neck. The longer he stood there, the more frustrated he became.

Cara nodded. "The wound was more than likely done with a kitchen knife or something similar with a short, thin, stiff blade about four to six inches long. The wound area has clean-cut edges, and the entry point is here, and the cut was done left to right," Cara said, pointing it out as she moved her hand across the body. "This would indicate a right-handed person."

"And is the cause of death still from blood loss?" Scott asked.

"Without a doubt. She was barely alive. There's discolouration above the ligature marks on both wrists. This would suggest she was alive, as blood was trapped above the ligature. There's no evidence of a struggle. By that I mean there are no scratches or bruising that would suggest she had been hit, and there are no skin scrapings beneath the nails. But we do have this." Cara moved to the feet of the cadaver and pushed each foot outwards. "We had the same type of oily residue on her heels as was found on the first victim. I've taken samples to send away for analysis, but I'm pretty confident that it will come back as a match to the composition of the first set of samples."

The evidence was further confirmation – not that he needed it – that this victim had been killed by the same perpetrator who'd committed the first crime. More importantly, both victims had more than likely been kept at the same location, which in Scott's view was around the Shoreham area.

Scott took a moment to cast his eye over the body. The picture of Rebecca on the incident board showed a vivacious, cheerful and attractive young woman. Now resting on the cold silver gurney, she'd lost the fresh and rosy pinkness of her skin tone. It had been replaced by a pale, ashy look much paler than the natural, living hue that she'd exuded in the picture.

When asked what a cadaver looked like on many occasions, Scott had tried to describe it. The closest explanation he could offer was it looked as though the person had just received a terrible shock and the blood had drained from their face. The light cream-coloured complexion stayed with them for about a week or so before the skin started to turn darker.

Thankfully, this cadaver hadn't reached that stage where the body turned black, as mould started to grow on it, much in the same way that mould grew on old bread.

Cara continued with her analysis and feedback. "Upon closer examination, I found many puncture marks in and around the lower abdomen and thigh region, conducive with repeated injections."

"A user?" Abby asked.

Cara shook her head. "Not on this occasion. She was a diabetic and reliant upon insulin injections."

The news caused Scott and Abby to exchange a surprised look.

Seeing the surprise on their faces, Cara continued, "I'm afraid so. Type one diabetics need regular insulin injections. There were early indications of diabetic damage to the organs, namely heart disease and damage to her kidneys, both of which are common in diabetics. The chances are her body ran out of insulin, which resulted in hyperglycaemia and then diabetic ketoacidosis, where the body basically runs out of insulin. This generally starts with an increased thirst from dehydration, headaches, problems concentrating and blurred vision before other symptoms kick in, like rapid breathing, confusion, and chronic fatigue."

Scott's mind raced as his stomach knotted. He felt saddened that they hadn't been able to find her in time, and angry at what the sick, twisted bastard had put her through since her capture.

Just before leaving, Cara had left them with a parting thought. She had gone on to say that the chances were that this particular victim was either semi-conscious or completely unconscious within twelve to twenty-four hours of her capture, so would have been spared the final gruesome moments of her life.

Scott turned to Abby as they were leaving the examination room. "Can you and the DCI head back to the station? I need to have a *word* with Cara about the cases."

Abby smiled and nodded. She silently mouthed 'good luck' as she disappeared through the doors.

45

Scott waited until Cara had finished. He paced around the visitors' room, stopping every few minutes to check the time on his watch. He was annoyed that he had been forced into this position by Berry.

It was a further twenty-minute wait before Cara wrapped up her examination and left her assistant to clean up. As she made her way to her office, Scott caught up with her.

"Cara, a quick word?"

Cara spun on her heel, surprised. "Scottie, what you doing here? Did you forget something?"

"No. No. I needed to talk to you about something, but I didn't want to interrupt you whilst you are doing your examination. I thought I'd wait until you'd finished."

Cara furrowed her brow. "You didn't have to wait. I would have stepped out of the examination and taken a quick break if it was urgent."

Scott led Cara to her office and shut the door behind them, beckoning her to take a seat beside him.

There was a mixture of surprise and curiosity on her face. She eyed him with suspicion.

"If you're going to propose to me, you could at least have picked a better setting," she teased.

Scott stroked her face. "No, that's not what I had in mind. It's about DCI Hermione Berry."

Cara tutted. "What has she done now? Is she still giving you grief?"

Scott licked his lips, to buy himself some time whilst he figured out how to say what he needed to say. He'd spent the last twenty minutes going through everything in his mind, but now as he sat in front of Cara, the words felt so jumbled in his head.

"Here goes. The DCI and I had the briefest of relationships back in Essex. It wasn't even a relationship; it was just a thing."

"Right, I didn't know that. You haven't mentioned her before. Nor did you say anything when she turned up in Brighton." Cara spoke matter-of-factly.

"Her arrival here was as much of a surprise to me as it was to anyone else. And the reason I haven't mentioned anything before was that she meant nothing to me. It was a silly mistake I made not long after joining the force. Too young and too many drinks and, well..."

Cara remained tight lipped as she crossed her arms over her chest and listened. Her expression gave nothing away.

Scott continued, telling Cara about the DI whom DCI Berry was involved with, the envelope of cash, his prints, and the doctored recording. Every minute felt like an hour as he explained the situation to Cara, who sat there in silence.

"She blackmailed you?" Cara finally said. "Either turn a blind eye and keep your mouth shut, or lose your job?"

Scott shrugged. "Pretty much. She heard about our case and decided to come down here and piss on my parade whilst jabbing me in the back with a cattle prod. The fact she's still got that recording... There's nothing I can do about that. It would be my word against hers, and I've got no evidence. Now she's winding me up, saying that she's considering Harvey's old job. There's no way I'm working for her."

Cara stood up and paced around the room, deep in thought.

"Did you have any feelings for her, then?"

Scott shook his head. He stood up too.

"And now?"

"I didn't feel anything for her then, and that hasn't changed. There's only one person I love and want to be with, and I'm looking at her now. Sorry I didn't tell you sooner, but I didn't know what to say."

Cara stepped in towards him. "What did we say about no more secrets?"

"I know, I know. I'm an idiot."

Cara ran a hand through her hair and groaned before looking up at the ceiling. "It's like our pasts keep coming back to screw with us." She looked at Scott. "Are you sure you don't feel even an itsy weenie tiny bit for her?"

"I swear on my life that I despise the woman. If I could put her on a train back to Essex today, I would. I'd even drive the train!"

Cara smiled softly before slipping her arms around Scott's waist. "What are you going to do?"

Scott sighed and blew out his cheeks. "I wish I knew. I really need to tell her to piss off, but that would only make her more dangerous. She likes a challenge. She likes to be in control." He pulled out a piece of paper and handed it to Cara.

Cara glanced at it and then Scott before looking at the address again. She shrugged, searching for an explanation.

"It's where Berry is staying. She left it on my desk and told me to join her there this evening or else."

Cara's eyes widened.

"You serious?" she shouted, waving the piece of paper in Scott's face. "I hope you told her to piss off."

Scott took the paper from Cara's hand and tore it in several pieces before throwing it into the wastepaper basket. "The fact that I won't turn up tonight will be a clear enough message. If she wants to drop me in it, then I'm going to drive to Essex and track down every single person with connections to her or that DCI. I'll dig up every ounce of dirt I can on them and then take it to the DPS."

Scott leant in and pulled Cara close to him. "I'm not going to let her or anyone else destroy my career or my relationship."

46

The man wasn't going to fail this time. Not capturing his project on the first attempt had frustrated him. He wasn't a man who coped well when things went wrong. He had spent weeks putting in the legwork. He'd identified suitable projects, built a strong understanding of their day-to-day lives. He knew the places they visited, the times they left their houses, and the times they returned. He knew their preferred style of dress, who their friends were, right down to what they enjoyed eating. Failure wasn't an option.

He was on a mission to enjoy the beauty of flame-haired vixens, and of course to make Sally – his Sally – proud of him. She had said on many occasions that with time, and the right level of care, he could perhaps look forward to experiencing a relationship. He was convinced that she had said that last bit as a subtle hint. With time *they* could look forward to a relationship. Him and his beautiful Sally. He loved that she gave him her undivided attention. When it was just them, nothing else seemed to matter. She never glanced at the clock or her phone. Her eyes were always focused on him.

He used to look forward to seeing her. He'd wait outside at least thirty minutes earlier than agreed. He'd pace nervously up and down the road. Excitement would bubble up inside him like he was a teenage boy waiting for his date to arrive.

The flurry of hysteria came in waves. Each wave was muted by a sense of serenity and calmness as his thoughts drifted back to the present.

He had a new project to acquire. He had found the perfect location where there was very little passing traffic, unlike his first attempt in Moulsecoomb. He needed to be somewhere he wouldn't look out of place.

His position was well concealed. The thunderous traffic of the A27 rumbled just metres away. It was hidden by dense shrubbery that formed a natural barrier between the busy dual carriageway and the side road where he had positioned his car. Adrenaline coursed through his veins like a rampaging river, yet on the outside he portrayed a look of calm.

This was only his second attempt at acquiring a new project in such a public place. The traffic on the other side of the hedgerow would be oblivious to his presence, and to his audacity. He was cunning and clever. He was about to prove that he was afraid of nothing.

He had watched her like he had done with the others. He had built up a pattern of her behaviour for weeks, including what times she cycled past and whom she talked to. He knew the routes she travelled. Her favourite meal was a quinoa and couscous salad with tomatoes, black beans and green onions. For breakfast she had the Sainsbury's basic range whole-wheat biscuits. After rummaging through her dustbin, he'd discovered that she preferred tampons to sanitary towels, and that she preferred Lil-Lets to Tampax as a brand. Oh yes, he knew everything about her.

He stood by the side of the road, at the junction for the turn into Stanmer Park. She was just moments away, and with the disguise that he'd donned this time, she would stop to help a person in need.

His pulse quickened when he saw her approach in the distance. He leant on to one crutch and used the other to flag her down. Her pace slowed, and she brought her bike to the kerb.

Sam Tearl greeted him with a warm smile. "Is everything okay?" Her voice was soft and slight.

"I'm so sorry. I've been on these crutches for weeks now, and I just needed to get out for some fresh air. I came over to the park," he said as he flicked his head in the direction of the park behind him. "When I returned to the car, I discovered a slow puncture. I can't believe my luck. First I damage my ankle and now this."

Sam looked beyond him to the blue Ford Mondeo parked a few metres behind with the boot lid open. "Oh bummer, is there anything I can do to help? Would you like me to call anyone?"

He offered the warmest of smiles. "That's very kind of you, luv, but in all honesty, it will be at least an hour before the recovery truck turns up. I'm just better off replacing the wheel with my spare. To be honest, I can pretty much handle most of it myself, but I could just do with a bit of help getting the tyre and jack out of my boot. If you could help me do that, I'd be really grateful."

Sam hesitated for a few moments, looking keen to continue her journey. She smiled and shrugged. "Well, I will certainly try. It might be a bit too heavy for me."

"That's all I can ask of you, luv," he reassured her as he swivelled on his crutch and hobbled back.

She dismounted and pushed the bike alongside them. "What did you do to your ankle?" she asked.

He feigned the effort it took to walk on crutches and blew out his cheeks. "You're going to laugh, luv, but my ankle gave way on the last few steps at home. I twisted it so badly that I damaged the Achilles tendon."

Sam winced and said, "Ouch, that does sound painful."

"Oh, trust me, it is. And now I struggle to get around. I haven't been out to do food shopping in weeks, and the house is a mess. It's surprising how something so minor can cause so much distress."

Sam nodded sympathetically as they stopped by the rear of his car. "Right, what do you want me to do?"

"If you could reach under the boot mat and grab the silver jack and the spare wheel. I can try to help with one hand whilst I steady myself on the other crutch."

"You sure that's a good idea?"

"Of course. I feel bad enough as it is. The least I can do is try to help you."

Sam looked around to find a suitable place to park her bike. She headed over to the nearby trees and rested it against a tree.

Upon her return, she retrieved the jack from beneath the mat and began to haul the large spare tyre out of the boot. It took some effort to begin with.

He reached in, keen to offer a degree of assistance. His mind raced.

With her bent over the way she was, his groin ached; he wanted her here and now. There was something about a woman bent over that he found deeply erotic. Perhaps it was that sense of control that he could have if he took her from behind.

Sam let out a couple of exasperated gasps as she toiled with the cumbersome object. "It's stuck in the well."

"You're doing so well; it's nearly out. Let me help you."

The man took a step backwards and glanced around. He needed to move away from this spot as quickly as possible.

He raised one crutch high above his head and brought it down on the back of her head with all the effort he could muster. The impact pushed her head forward, causing it to strike the wheel rim. She slumped into the boot, unconscious. He dropped his crutches and immediately grabbed her around the waist. He groaned as he hauled the rest of her body into the boot and pushed her knees up into the foetal position. Speed was of the essence; there was always the risk that at any moment a car or some groundsman would pass by.

He decided to leave the bike against the tree. He drove out. The Mondeo slowly slipped out of the side road and turned right towards Brighton. He breathed a sigh of relief. His audacious plan had worked. A warm sense of fulfilment and contentment washed over him as his body finally relaxed.

Mission accomplished.

He pulled up the roller shutters on the workshop to reverse his car back in before closing them to hide his presence. In the semi-darkness of his sanctuary, he could relax.

The box had been prepared in readiness for her arrival. All traces of its former inhabitant had been wiped away with copious amounts of bleach wipes. It was spotless and sanitised.

He took his time to strip her naked. She was small and petite, he guessed no taller than five-foot two inches, which made her light and easy to manoeuvre. It would prove an easy task to place her inside the metal box later.

He now wanted to explore her body while she lay unconscious.

He began by cutting a small lock of her hair and placing it in a small trinket box to go alongside the other souvenirs he'd gathered.

She has smaller, more pert breasts than the other two projects, almost adolescent looking.

But she did share similar qualities to Rebecca and Hailey. Her skin was smooth and soft. Her body was toned, her hair flame-red. He liked her broad mouth and fuller lips.

With his finger, he traced the outline of her body, following the outer edge. He stroked the firmness of her belly and admired the thin landing strip of pubic hair.

He stroked her thin, lean legs, which led to pretty feet that were suddenly spoilt by unpainted toenails. He snarled in disgust.

How could she have not prepared for me, when she knew I was meeting her?

47

Alexis wasn't too sure what time it was, or how long she'd been asleep. *Forty-five minutes? Perhaps two hours?* She couldn't think straight. Her mind felt foggy, her head pounded, and her body ached. She felt like she'd been hit by a bus; the throbbing headache almost suggested that she had.

How much had she drunk? Had someone spiked her drink? Had she eaten something that had wiped her out?

She could barely remember the last thing she'd done, but here she was under a duvet facing the wall in her student bedroom in halls. Was she dreaming? She couldn't tell; everything was a hazy blur. Was her mind playing tricks on her?

Yet her boyfriend, Simon, had his arm around her, cupping her breast. He was curled into her back, their knees tucked into one another. Her back tickled from his hairy chest, and the warmth from his breath rushed past her ear. His erect penis nestled against her arse cheeks, gently pushing rhythmically against her. Her eyes closed for a brief sensual moment as she welcomed Simon's closeness.

Chest! Hairy chest!

Her eyes sprang open, wide with terror and confusion.

Simon doesn't have a hairy chest!

Her body froze. Perhaps this was a dreadful freaky dream. Her eyes tried hard to adjust to the darkened room; she looked around, desperate to focus on something familiar.

She flinched when the person behind her groaned.

Alexis tried to move her arms, but something stopped her. Her palms were pressed firmly together. Her wrists burnt the harder she tried to move them.

A deep laugh rocked her ears. "Hello there, beautiful," came the voice from behind her.

With every ounce of energy she thrashed out and tried to scream, but her lips wouldn't move. Something was pressed on them. *Tape.*

Everything became a dark blur as she was flipped onto her back. A heavy hand pressed down on her throat as he ripped the tape from her lips.

Freddie laughed as he straddled her. She flailed her legs in an attempt to free herself, but he only pressed down harder on her throat. Her eyes bulged as her pulse throbbed in her temples. White spots clouded her vision. He used his knees to force her thighs apart. She had little energy to fight as he tried to enter her.

She needed to escape. She needed help now. From somewhere deep inside, she emitted a piercing shrill, followed by another.

Freddie gave her a backhanded slap to silence her.

THIS WASN'T WORKING out the way he'd hoped. The lube sat untouched by the side of the bed. He hadn't had time to film anything. He'd screwed up by taking the tape off her mouth.

Now others were banging on the door, a mixture of curiosity and concern from those on the other side.

He needed her now. She wasn't going to ruin it for him, and neither were the do-gooders in the corridor. His mind raced with a heady concoction of fear, excitement and possessiveness. The more he attempted to push into her, the more desperate he became.

"Shut up," he yelled and slapped her again.

By now the commotion in the corridor had reached fever pitch. Gentle shoves against the door were replaced with more forceful attempts. The door rocked in its frame and threatened to give way at any moment.

He leant in and bit Alexis hard on the shoulder. She screamed.

The door gave way when two men shoulder-charged it one final time.

People flooded in. Some pulled Freddie off, pinning him to the floor, whilst others tended to Alexis, her eyes fixed wide in abject fear. They ushered her away wrapped in a duvet as they tried to calm her hysterical screams.

Anger flooded through his body as he lay face down, a knee in his back firmly pinning him to the spot.

He hated failure.

48

Silence enveloped Scott, lost in his own thoughts for a moment as he struggled to clear his mind. Tiredness had robbed him of all energy that morning. The few hours' sleep last night and the second cup of strong coffee had done little to jolt him into some form of normality. He gazed into the bottom of his cup, his thoughts in shreds, the knot in the pit of his stomach growing as the minutes ticked on.

"Morning!" Abby's bright and cheerful voice came out of nowhere.

Scott barely looked up and mustered a smile when Abby bounced into his office with a spring in her step.

He groaned. "You're far too bright and cheerful at this time of the morning. That can only mean one thing. You slept out again last night?"

Abby tapped the side of her nose. "That would be for me to know, and for you to find out, *Detective*."

Scott would normally have a rebuke already lined up, but all he could offer was a friendly, "Huh."

Abby tilted her head. "You okay? How did it go yesterday with Cara?"

"Better than I had hoped for. We talked. I'm not letting the DCI ruin my career or relationship. Berry gave me an ultimatum last night." Scott flapped his hand in the air when Abby frowned. "Long story, I'll tell you later. Anyway, I ignored it...so let's see what she's going to throw at me today."

"I'm here if you need me. Well, it's good news about Freddie Coltrane's arrest. It looks like he was caught in the act last night. It will be interesting to see how he talks his way out of this one."

Scott nodded weakly. It was good news, but at this precise moment he just wanted to be left alone. Tiredness and the emotional stress had sapped his mental and physical energy.

Abby suggested breakfast, which he kindly declined and asked for a rain check. She left him in peace and breezed out.

Scott stared at the ceiling for what felt like hours but in reality was no more than a few minutes.

His eyes felt heavy enough to allow him to drift off to sleep. "Jesus, so help me God." He groaned.

"You need more than God to help you out," Berry announced as she walked into his office and closed the door.

An uneasy silence filled the room. The tension in the air made it hard for Scott to breathe. He glanced at her before he returned his gaze to the bottom of his coffee cup. He could sense her eyes drilling into the top of his head. She was known for her cold, calculating stare, which unnerved many who dealt with her. But he refused to be intimidated.

Berry walked around to his side of the desk and ran her fingers lightly across his shoulders. His body stiffened beneath her touch.

Berry leant over and came close to his ear. "I'm disappointed in you, Scott. I thought you had so much more sense.

All it's going to take is one word from me and you're out of here."

Her voice was soft, her breath warm as she spoke with a chilling, determined softness.

"Imagine how Meadows would react if he found out that you came on to me. And you tried to assault me when I pushed you off. Between you and me, I don't think they'll give you time to clear your desk and say goodbye to your wonderful team. Incidentally, I think I'll quite enjoy having a team like yours under my command."

Scott breathed hard as he fought to stay calm. His eyelids twitched, and his hands curled into fists. Scott pushed his chair back abruptly and stood up, catching Berry off guard. They stood nose to nose, their eyes locked in their own battle of wills.

"Do your worst, DCI Berry. I've got a killer to catch. I'm not scared of you. If you're going to take me down, then you're coming with me. And that's a promise. I still have plenty of connections back in Essex. How long do you think it will take before I uncover enough dirt on you to bury you for good?"

"Fighting talk," she cooed.

"Don't mess with me." Scott raised a brow and called her bluff. "You may have recorded *that* conversation for insurance, for a rainy day, but did I do the same?"

She was just about to respond when the door flew open.

Abby raced in without looking and paused mid-step. The close proximity of Scott and Berry, their faces just a few inches apart, confused her.

"Um, sorry to barge in. We've just had a report of a third student being abducted."

49

Abby dashed back to the incident board, where Helen was putting up the details of the latest missing person. Scott followed a few paces behind. DCI Berry followed at the rear, her arms crossed, her walk slow and measured.

Helen turned and began to relay the details that had been passed through to her from the control room.

"Sam Tearl didn't show up for a pre-planned meeting with a friend on campus yesterday. They had agreed to meet late afternoon, between four p.m. and five p.m. By five thirty p.m. he had sent several text messages and tried her number. She didn't reply to any of them. She's twenty years old, and as you can see from her picture," Helen said, tapping the new image on the incident board with her pen, "another redhead."

Scott studied the pictures of all three women and bit his bottom lip as he stuffed his hands in his pockets. "And what was she studying?"

"She was coming to the end of her second year in business and finance."

"So she wouldn't have been in any of the other classes with Hailey or Rebecca. How does she normally get to campus?"

Helen checked her notes. "She usually travels by bicycle. She shares a student house with several others in town. Her friend Ketan Amin became increasingly worried. When he hadn't heard from her by six p.m., he decided to retrace the path she normally took just in case something had happened to her. He found her bike leant against a tree."

"And that's when he called it in?" Abby asked.

"Yes, skip, shortly after that," Helen said. "They have a lot of mutual friends, so he called them just in case she had forgotten or had lost her phone. When no one had heard from her, he became increasingly worried. He panicked. The poor lad is beside himself, according to officers who attended."

Scott said, "Okay, team, do the usual. Build up a timeline of her movements in the hours leading up to four p.m. Speak to her friends, look at social media accounts, visit her digs. Look for any clues that might explain her disappearance. However, we can assume that she may have fallen victim to our man. Have a look to see if any of her personal possessions are still lying around. And whilst you're there, grab a recent picture of her and some hair fibres." He hoped on this occasion that they wouldn't need to do any DNA analysis. "Okay, you crack on with it. Abby and I are going downstairs to interview Freddie Coltrane."

FREDDIE COLTRANE LOOKED dishevelled and agitated as he sat in interview room one. As expected, Beecham his solicitor was present. He too looked just as uncomfortable as his client. Abby did the introductions for the tape recorder and cautioned Freddie.

Scott studied Freddie's face. A lack of sleep and what appeared to be evidence of a scuffle had left him looking decidedly battered and bruised. His clothes had been removed for forensic analysis. He now wore a white paper suit, which he complained was uncomfortable.

"Freddie, it looks like things haven't gone your way this time. Can you tell us what happened last night?"

Freddie glanced at Beecham, who gave him one shake of his head.

"No comment," he said in a croaky voice.

"Did you go out with the intention of finding a female you could engage in sexual activity with?"

"No comment."

"When you were arrested, they noticed that your pupils were dilated, and there were traces of a white substance on your table. They believed that you were in possession of a controlled class A substance, possibly cocaine. It is for that reason that you were required to give a sample, which you consented to. They took a saliva swab from you on the spot. The DrugWipe tested positive for cocaine. Did you give Alexis Deacon cocaine with the sole intention of incapacitating her?"

Freddie sniggered and slouched in his chair. "No comment."

Scott crossed his arms and glanced at Abby for a brief moment. "Here's my thoughts, Freddie. I think you've gone too far this time. Your solicitor, your parents, the vice chancellor, in fact, no one can help you on this occasion. Alexis has pressed charges against you. She's alleged that you tried to rape her. The police doctor has confirmed evidence of bruising commonly found in cases of sexual assault. She also felt very unwell and drowsy when she woke. She believes that something was put in her drink. Can you confirm this?"

"No comment."

Scott leant over the table and splayed his hands out in front of him. "Freddie, you're a sick, twisted individual who gets his kicks from targeting women and carrying out violent sexual acts on them. What does it do for you? Does it make you feel special? Important? Or does it inflate that ego of yours further?"

Freddie raised his eyes to meet Scott's. Scott had clearly touched a raw nerve, as the younger man's chest heaved.

Scott continued, "I put it to you that you went out with the sole intention of targeting a lone female. You plied her with drugs so that you could take her back to your bedroom with the intention of having non-consensual sex. Does it make you feel like a man? Because from where I'm sitting, you're just a boy."

Freddie sprang to his feet; his chair flew back several feet. A surprised Beecham practically choked on his own breath. Scott and Abby remained unfazed, fully expecting a response. "I'm – not – a – boy." He snarled the words, spittle flying across the table. "She deserved it. She wanted it."

"Sit down, little man, or you're about to find four officers sitting on you within seconds," Scott instructed. He held his hand over the red DaDo panic strip attached to the wall. "Your call…"

Freddie glared at Scott before lowering himself back down.

Abby took over. "According to Mistress Claire, you like blood, pain and this notion of being cut. Is that what you wanted to do to Alexis?"

A contemptuous laugh echoed around the room. "Oh, look, the monkey talks. Is the organ grinder having a rest?"

Abby pushed on. “Another student has gone missing. Sam Tearl. Do you know her?”

Freddie looked up at the ceiling in feigned contemplation. He shook his head. “Nah, the name doesn’t ring a bell. Should it?”

Scott took over. “The white substance we found has been sent away for forensic analysis. We’ve also taken a blood sample from Alexis to identify whether there are any class A drugs in her system. We’ve also taken swabs from her. And we’re fairly confident that we’ll find traces of your DNA on her. But for the time being, we’re charging you with the possession of a class A controlled substance and the intent to commit a sexual offence, in this case rape and common assault.”

Scott sat back, pleased with the outcome. They had the victim, forensic evidence and witnesses. Freddie wouldn’t be going anywhere for a long time.

50

Scott returned from interviewing and charging Freddie Coltrane to find Berry in an unusually happy and excited mood. She stood in front of the team, a beaming smile spread across her face. "Well done, everyone. You've been doing an amazing job in very difficult circumstances. If we crack this, the drinks are on me."

The offer of an alcoholic reward was met with a delighted response from the team, Mike being the most vocal.

The joviality died down when Scott and Abby walked up, their faces fixed with inquisitiveness.

"What did we miss?" Scott asked.

"Lots of progress for a change, thanks to the team," Berry said. "Three units have been identified that had marine engineering-based businesses in the past. They will need searching. Two are based in Shoreham, one in Brighton. We've also got a very promising lead from SCAS. Helen, do you want to brief the rest of the team on the post-mortem report on Rebecca?"

Helen nodded as she shuffled her papers into order. "There were raised sodium levels and traces of diazepam found in her blood. She had some evidence of diseased organs as a result of her diabetes. Her insulin levels were life-threateningly low, which led to severe dehydration."

"Any history of her using diazepam or being prescribed it?" Scott asked.

"No, guv."

"We can assume that the diazepam may have been used as some form of sedative," Scott added.

Helen nodded once in agreement. "There were cuts and grazes to her body and feet. Soil samples taken from her heels matched the soil where she was found. The oily substance also found on her heels was a direct match to that found on Hailey Bratton. Dr Hall also confirmed in her report that an ammonia-based compound was evident on the surface of her skin. In particular, the areas that showed high concentrations of irritation."

Scott processed the information. "So once again the murderer did their best to remove potential traces of DNA. They're just taunting us."

"Any sign of sexual assault?" Abby asked.

Helen flicked through her notes. "There were fresh abrasions inside the vaginal canal. There was no bruising on her inner thighs or signs of forced penetration. She confirmed that Rebecca Thorne died from massive blood loss."

Scott pointed at Mike to speak next.

"I've just been covering a few loose ends. I can confirm now that all staff on campus have been vetted and cleared. However, as I was saying to DCI Berry just shortly before you arrived, we have the records from SCAS on the psychiatrist from Essex."

"Promising?" Scott asked.

Berry interrupted. "Definitely, they have come up trumps for the team. You've done well there, Mike. You just kept pushing with SCAS, and they turned stuff around really quickly due to your persistence."

Mike smiled; his red, fat cheeks flushed with pride.

Scott ignored Berry's attempt at scoring a few brownie points with the team.

"Yes, guv," Mike said. "They went through her cases going back several years. They focused on any cases where clients had issues with women or were known to harm or stalk them. They also looked at patients with common mental health issues involving self-harm, depersonalisation, voices in their head and schizophrenia. There were five names that they came back with. I passed them on to Raj so he could cross-reference." Mike looked at Raj to carry on the feedback.

Thanking Mike, Raj continued the feedback. "I took those five names and crossed them against hospitals in the Essex region. Only one of those names popped up. Brian Hopper. He saw Sally Martin for three years. He was prescribed diazepam and lithium carbonate from the mental health unit in Colchester. He was diagnosed with bipolar. Hospital records confirm that he has not renewed his prescription in over four years."

Scott's mind was ticking over at warp speed as he digested the news. "So unless he's getting his meds from somewhere else, he could be unstable?"

Raj nodded. "That's what the hospital feared, too. This is where it gets more interesting, guv. Sally reported him to the police for harassment and stalking, but no further action was taken other than a warning, despite her repeated calls and concerns. Essex Police didn't see it as a problem, as no harm had come to her."

The team exchanged discreet glances whilst Berry remained tight-lipped. They would all know that Berry would have had knowledge of this incident at the time of her disappearance.

"Anything on his whereabouts?" Scott asked, deciding not to push that point.

Raj shook his head. "No fixed abode. He was in Essex but disappeared four years ago. Sally's notes highlighted that she authorised a doubling of his dose on the day she disappeared. Hopper was in her diary for that morning."

There was a brief silence as the team reflected and absorbed the latest credible information.

Scott stood by the incident board and looked at the young faces. He almost gave them an apologetic look, wishing that he'd been able to stop the killer before more victims after Hailey had lost their lives.

"Raj, get his picture out to the press. Make it an urgent appeal for help with our enquiries. Speak to the press officer, to word it in a way that doesn't scare him off. The last thing we want is him going underground."

Scott had one of his gut feelings again. The net was closing in, and Brian Hopper was their chief suspect.

51

By midday, the earlier enthusiasm had turned to quiet optimism. Hopper's image had been released to the online press channels, which were quick to start publicising the appeal. However, Berry was unhappy with the rate of progress to track down Hopper. Berry wasn't one of those officers who liked to follow, preferring instead to lead. Scott taking charge of the new line of enquiry was likely ruffling her feathers.

As Scott walked back to his office, Berry followed him in hot pursuit, vocal about how she felt.

He entered his office, and Berry barked orders at him.

"Scott, we need to draft in a few more officers to speed things up. I'm sure that the team are doing the best they possibly can, but it's not good enough. Meadows will want concrete action quicker than you can hum the national anthem. If you can't speed this case up, then I will."

"With all due respect, ma'am, my officers are working flat out," Scott shouted back.

Berry's shrill voice punctured the air. "It's not enough, Scott."

"I think I know my officers a damn sight better than you, ma'am."

A stunned silence fell upon the team outside, clearly uncomfortable about the heated discussion taking place in Scott's office.

Scott closed the door to his office. Berry continued to argue with him. "You need to get answers quickly."

"May I remind you that before your arrival, we were doing absolutely fine. If anything, we need to be asking Essex police questions about the missed opportunities to save Sally Martin and stop Brian Hopper whilst *you* were in charge!"

"Do you call losing an officer fine? And from where I'm standing, that was one almighty fuck-up that you were in charge of."

Berry jerked the door open and stormed out. The team sat in stunned silence, exchanging glances that seemed to suggest "What just happened?"

Abby instructed the rest of the team to crack on with their work, then marched into Scott's office and folded her arms in consternation.

Scott raised his hands in surrender, feeling tired and weary. "If you're going to have a go, then join the back of the queue. I think I've had enough for today."

"No, I'm not going to have a go at you. You're coming with me for a cup of coffee, and I won't take no for an answer."

STARBUCKS WASN'T the usual type of coffee shop that Scott and Abby visited. They were forced to weave in and out of the many prams and buggies that were gathered around the huddles of mums having their weekly catch-up.

The incessant chatter and babies screaming only added to Scott's pounding headache. Abby had grabbed a skinny caramel latte for herself, and an espresso shot for Scott in the hope it would spark him awake.

An uneasy silence hung between the pair. Abby stared at Scott, trying to read his mind. She had known him long enough to know that he was behaving out of character. She had always known him to be strong, assertive and fair, qualities that he had displayed in both his personal and professional life.

Cupping her latte in both hands, she rested her elbows on the table. "As your friend, what is up with you? I'm worried."

Scott slouched in his chair and shook his head.

Abby raised an eyebrow. "Is that it? Is that all you've got?"

"I'm sorry," Scott offered.

Abby pulled a sad face as the edges of her mouth turned down. "Don't apologise to me. If anything, you should apologise to yourself. Listen, I care about you. You're my friend as well as my colleague, and for my sins, my boss. If I didn't care, I wouldn't be sitting in the middle of a coffee shop, listening to kids screaming in stereo. This is off the record...I want to help."

Scott stared at the ceiling. "Off the record?"

"Cross my heart, or you can have all the chocolate in my chocolate drawer at home."

Scott rubbed his chin and grimaced.

"So what else has she done?" Abby pushed.

"She basically told me to sleep with her, and if I didn't, she'd go and tell Meadows that I had been uncooperative in the sharing of this case. If I didn't play ball, she was going to say that I tried it on with her one night and that she had to fight me off."

"No way. She really has a screw loose. What a cow!" Abby spewed in anger. "You can't let her get away with this... Wait, you didn't..."

Scott shook his head. "Last night she wanted me to go and visit her at the hotel." Scott stared at a spot beyond Abby.

"Tell me you didn't go?" Abby pleaded.

"Nope. That's why I stayed back to talk to Cara. I told her everything. And because I didn't play along with Berry's games, she's pissed off with me." Scott laughed weakly.

"You have to go and tell Meadows. Explain the situation to him. You can't let her get away with this."

"No chance. Meadows is already in Berry's pocket. He can't praise her highly enough. He's even discussed the possibility of her taking Harvey's post. Who are they going to believe – DCI Berry, who's got a spotless record and is a high achiever, or a DI who lost an officer on his watch and who still hasn't got over the loss of his family?"

Abby sat back in her chair. "So you're going to let her walk all over you?"

"No chance. I'm calling her bluff. She has more to lose than I have. Trust me, I'm on her case. I'm sure I can dig up enough dirt on her if she wants to play that game!"

52

"There's nothing nicer than the female form. And you are unique with your milky white skin and flame-red hair. You have vibrancy, a fire, and essence that many can't come close to matching."

He had gone to great lengths to enjoy this moment with her. Stripped naked and lying beside her on an inflatable mattress, he studied her body. She was lean and taut, just the way he liked it. She had a thinner frame than Rebecca and Hailey, but he still relished the opportunity to explore her body further.

He stroked her stomach; the fine downy hair added warmth to his touch. He leant in and breathed in her scent that still lingered on her skin. The hint of watermelon soothed and calmed him. A body spray from Hollister – Crescent Bay Mist.

His fingers trembled as he gave the lightest of touches to her skin down one side. He loved following the curve of her body as it tucked into her waist before moving out to her hips. He studied the thin line of bright, fiery, orange pubic hair that nestled between her legs. His erect penis twitched and jerked as it rested on her thigh. His heart raced. His breathing was rapid and deep.

He nestled his face in the side of her neck and licked her skin. He moved in closer and enjoyed the warmth of her flesh on his skin. Their torsos and legs connected as one. She groaned. Her bound hands and feet left her defenceless as he took his time to enjoy these first few precious moments with her.

He cut her, then lowered his head and licked the beads of deep red blood that had burst to the surface of the open wound. His lids flickered in response to the taste of her; the sensual act whisked him away to a place of deep, dark eroticism. His penis responded with a jerk and released over her thigh.

Guttural screams erupted from her throat as she flinched. She thrashed her head violently. She was powerless to fight him off.

He smiled and said, "At least you've got a bit more spirit than the other two. Sally thinks so too; that's why we chose you. I guess you like me as much as I like you, eh?" He pushed her matted hair away from her face so he could admire her clean, natural beauty.

"It's not your time yet. Sally and I are hoping that you will stay with us a bit longer so that we can really get to know you. I think it's really important to get to know someone first. What do you think, Sally?"

A cold, eerie silence lingered between them as his eyes bored into her, looking through her, deep into the depths of her mind and soul.

"You see, there's no turning back for you now. You belong to us. The moment you fell for me was the moment you gave yourself to us so we could share and enjoy in your youthful beauty. I'm going to enjoy exploring every inch of you," he muttered under his breath. "I'm going to start at the top of your head and work my way right down to your toes. When I'm finished with you, you'll be damaged goods. I'm going to do things to you that you never dreamt possible."

Tears spilled from the corners of her eyes as she begged for her safety. "Please...please stop. Please don't hurt me. I promise I won't say a word to anyone else if you let me go. I don't want to..." She choked out a sob; spittle bubbled from her mouth. Her eyes were fixed wide in terror.

"Shh, shh. There's no need to get upset. Tears won't help you now, and your pleas...well, they're pretty lame," he said, smiling and stroking her face in an attempt to calm her. "You'll be fast asleep and won't even know when it's over."

His words sparked further terror, and she recoiled from him. Her body heaved with sobs.

He smiled as a pool of liquid formed between her legs.

He pinched her cheeks with one hand and parted her lips ever so slightly. With his other hand, he tipped the contents of the teaspoon into her mouth. He placed a hand over her mouth until he was sure she had swallowed the white powder.

"It's time to rest," he said gently.

53

Yesterday now seemed a blur as Scott scrolled through his emails on his phone the next morning whilst holding a coffee and croissant that he had grabbed on the way to work. The team had worked hard and progressed the case significantly. It had kept Berry off his back, which in itself was a blessing. He wasn't quite sure if he could handle any more grief from Berry, or Abby for that matter.

Scott had taken work home and had sat up until the early hours going through the case files. He'd pulled himself away during the evening to spend a few hours with Cara. The nature of the job meant that holding down a relationship was challenging at the best of times. They had grabbed a fish and chips supper from Wolfies of Hove and had cosied up in front of the TV whilst they watched a movie and enjoyed dinner.

It was moments like those that Scott savoured the most, watching Cara sprawled out across the sofa with her head on his lap. He'd stroked her hand whilst they enjoyed their togetherness. The movie had cast light and dark hypnotic shadows that danced on the walls around them at the same time that Cara had dozed off.

Overnight, Raj had updated the case files online. He'd been able to confirm that following his enquiries, Hopper had been to hospitals in Essex and the Royal Sussex in Brighton on numerous occasions to try to obtain his medication. However, when doctors had wanted to question him further, he'd become agitated and made off before hospital security could attend.

This information alone suggested that Hopper needed to be found if for nothing more than to be eliminated from their enquiries.

Several other emails caught Scott's attention. The first was in relation to some discreet enquiries he'd made over in Essex. He'd followed up on a hunch about the way Berry and the Essex team had conducted the enquiry into the disappearance of Sally Martin. He'd requested a copy of the investigation file. Whilst reviewing the file, Scott had questioned the thoroughness of the procedures followed and the documented findings. To him there were some glaring gaps in the way that the investigation had been managed, and crucial information hadn't been recorded.

His hunch had paid off, and he glared at his screen.

He scanned the rest of his emails. Following the release of Hopper's image to the press, a steady stream of phone calls had come in from members of the public. Sightings of a man matching Hopper's description were recorded in Hove, Brighton, Shoreham and as far as Hassocks. Most would be dead ends but would need a follow-up by his team.

What caught Scott's interest was several students had reported seeing a man matching Hopper's description on Stony Mere Way adjacent to the A27 Lewis Road, and close to Sussex University. Scott knew the road well. It was used as the main access road for students and ran parallel to the busy dual carriageway. He forwarded the reports on to Raj and requested that he follow them up to gain further information.

His optimism rose as Scott examined further reports that could help find the whereabouts of Hopper, as well as locate the missing student, Sam Tearl.

One particular report piqued Scott's interest. It was from a letting agent. He decided to call the agent himself.

A well-spoken gentleman answered on the third ring. "Good morning, PPS Lettings, Devish Patel speaking, how can I help?"

"Mr Patel, this is Detective Inspector Baker from Brighton CID. I'm following up on a call that you made to us about our press appeal. I understand that you believe you recognised the person in the picture?"

There was a slight hesitation before Devish spoke. "I'm not going to get into...trouble, am I? Because of...what I'm telling you?" he said, stumbling over the words.

"It depends on what you're going to say, Mr Patel; however, I can assure you that anything you do say to me will be treated in the strictest confidence. Provided that you haven't broken the law and committed an offence, I can't see any problems."

"Okay, okay," he replied rapidly. "That fella in the picture looks familiar, but he used a different name. He said his name was Tom Atkins, not Brian Hopper. But if I'm honest, he looks exactly like your man."

"And where did you see him?" Scott asked as he scribbled 'Tom Atkins' on his notepad and circled it a few times.

"He rented an industrial unit a couple of weeks back. To be honest, we've got a few of them available, and they've sat idle for the past two years. If they're left unoccupied, there are more chances of them being vandalised and broken into. And of course, we're not making money if they sit idle. Anyway, he said he needed to store some stuff there because he was moving, and wanted to pay in cash, with no questions asked."

"And as far as you're concerned, he's still using it?"

"As far as I know, Inspector. I gave him a set of keys, and I haven't had them back. I can only assume that, yes, he is using it."

Scott thanked Mr Patel and grabbed the address of the unit before hanging up.

His stomach twisted with excitement. He had a good feeling about that lead and had just got in to brief the rest of the team when DCI Berry walked into his office. They exchanged a silent stare. Coldness dominated her eyes as they bored into him. The long silence between them seemed as much a battle of wills as it was about who had the stronger determination to stand their ground.

"It's still not too late to change your mind, Scott. I think we could be good together, and our connection could open up a lot of doors for you. I could put in a good word for you, and you could have Harvey's job. And you could put in a good word for me, and I could go after Meadows's job. Between you and me, I heard that Meadows is eyeing up a role at HQ."

Scott grinned. He felt more self-assured than he had done in days. Perhaps it was the pep talk with Abby, or the call he'd just had that ignited a fire in his belly.

"It's always about you, isn't it? You're not worried about the case or me. It's just about where you're headed and how fast you can get there. You've charmed Meadows, and now you want to stab him in the back. And me? I'm just collateral damage. You used me once, and I was young and naïve enough to fall for it. But trust me, you have a lot more to lose than me if you decide to kick off."

Berry narrowed her eyes. "As I said before, Scott, who are they going to believe? A DI or a DCI?"

"With all due respect, *ma'am*, you've fucked up, and I'm just biding my time."

She sneered. "You haven't got the balls."

"Try me," Scott replied as he breezed past her towards the incident board.

54

With a nervous energy coursing through his veins, Scott raced to the incident board. "Listen up, team. Following the press release on Hopper, I've received a very promising lead."

The team shuffled their chairs to face the board, a mix of curiosity and excitement lighting their faces.

"We've had a possible sighting of Brian Hopper, and more importantly, the sighting could lead us to finding Sam Tearl. A letting agent called in last night. He's fairly certain that a man matching the description of Brian Hopper rented a commercial unit in Lancing from him for cash, no questions asked. That would make sense, as the unit isn't too far from where the bodies of Hailey and Rebecca were discovered. What's more interesting is that this commercial unit was used in the past to house an engineering firm servicing outboard motors for yachts and speedboats."

Scott turned to the board, grabbed a marker and added a few notes whilst the conversation was fresh in his mind. "If that's the case, that would tie in with the oil traces found on the heels of Hailey and Rebecca. What's also encouraging is that several students noticed a man matching Hopper's description standing in Stony Mere Way on the day that Sam went missing."

With excitement in his voice, Scott continued to relay information about Hopper's visits to the hospitals. "This could be our man. In fact, I'm certain he's *our man*," Scott added as he glanced towards the back of the room where Berry sat stony-faced and sombre.

Mike said, "Guv, we've been scouring the CCTV footage on the night of Rebecca's disappearance. And we've finally managed to spot a car pulling out of King Place and turning right up North Street. It was too dark to get any clear visual on the driver, and the image is quite grainy. I've checked, and nothing was noticed on ANPR anywhere either, so we can only track the car as far as Dyke Road. After that, we can't confirm the direction the car travelled in, but it looks like they wanted to steer clear of the cameras. It's a Ford Mondeo. One of the students saw a blue car parked in Stony Mere Way not far from where they saw the man matching Hopper's description. Could it be the same car?"

"Excellent, great work, Mike. That lends more weight to my belief it's our man."

There was a general consensus amongst the team, who nodded in agreement. "What's the next step, guv?" Helen asked.

"I've already had uniform do a drive-by of the industrial unit. There's no sign of his car, and the shutters are down. That's not to say he's not inside. Clearly, I don't want them banging on the door and scaring him off. I've instructed them to maintain observation from a discreet distance. I don't want to pussyfoot around, so we need to head down there now and go in hard and quick."

Mike was already out of his chair and grabbing his stab vest before Scott had finished briefing the team, much to the amusement of others. Whenever there was a bit of action, Mike was always at the front of the line.

"Hold on, Mike. I need you to arrange for the tactical entry team to follow us down in convoy with a dog unit. Our aim is twofold. Once the tactical team have gained entry for us, firstly, we need to locate Hopper and isolate him. Secondly, we need to look for Sam Tearl. There's no guarantee that she is being held there. However, the chances are that wherever Hopper is, Sam Tearl will be."

Scott looked around at his eager team. The last time they had been out in an operation, they had lost one of their own. As he scanned their excited faces, he couldn't help but still feel responsible for Sian's loss. Today, he was again in charge of his team's safety.

"Now, I don't need to remind you about the importance of putting your safety first. We stay in pairs. Under *no* circumstances do we split up. Hopper is dangerous. He is suspected of killing two women and abducting a third. He also has mental health issues and, as far as we can gather, has not been taking his prescribed medication. That would suggest that there is a strong possibility that when we discover him, he may be unstable.

"I've spoken to the police doctor, and she's informed me that someone displaying those types of mental health issues can appear very calm and rational. But they tend to flip from the slightest of triggers. Those triggers can vary from person to person. When we find him, you need to approach with caution. Equally, he could be completely unhinged and just come at us with a weapon. So please remain vigilant. Mike and Abby will both go armed with tasers and will only use them as a last resort, understand?"

They both nodded, Mike more reluctantly than Abby.

"Any questions?" A collective silence from the team suggested that they were all ready to go. With that, a frenzied flurry of officers flew around their desks as they grabbed phones, stab vests, utility belts, and batons.

Scott felt the anticipation and buzz. The energy in the room pulsated and quickened as they raced out the door.

Berry held back and grabbed Scott's arm as he was about to pass. "Scott, as the senior officer here, you should have consulted me with regard to what you had planned next. I'll come with you and take over when we arrive on location."

Scott glanced at her grip around his arm.

He brought his eyes level with hers. "With all due respect, ma'am, I'm the SIO here, and this is my patch. If you've got a problem with it, then you're more than welcome to take it up with Meadows. Tag along if you want to, but you're not running this operation."

55

He knelt by the cold steel box and gripped the sides as he peered in. He admired her beauty once again. Curled up in the foetal position, she looked so young, delicate and adoringly sweet.

How could anyone find her unattractive? How could anyone hurt such a delicate and stunning beauty?

Her skin felt soft as he ran his finger down her arm. He tingled with excitement as he touched her again. "Sally was just saying that she thought you were a keeper. You know, I think she likes you more than the other two. Sadly, it looks like they found me quicker than I thought. It was only a matter of time, but it's interrupted our chances of being happy."

He shuddered as a cold shiver raced down his spine.

Perhaps she led them here? Perhaps I wasn't as careful as I'd hoped?

Whatever the reason, he knew that they were coming for him. He would have his time again. He could wait for another time where he could start again in a different part of the country where no one knew him.

Somewhere remote. Maybe a farmhouse or an outbuilding where I won't be disturbed. Wales? Scotland?

As he stood, he stretched his back to relieve the tightness, then glanced over his shoulder at the shuttering.

"I'll be back, my lovely, with my final present for you." He headed for the stairs that led to the basement.

56

Pedestrians paused as the convoy of four police vehicles raced through the Old Steine and out on to the Kingsway. Cars frantically parted as the dog unit led the charge, followed by two CID pool cars and the tactical entry team at the rear in a people carrier. Their sirens wailed; the sound echoed and bounced off the tall buildings around them.

Scott, Abby and DCI Berry trailed in the first pool car, with Mike, Raj and Helen following in the second. The cars weaved in and out of the traffic as they raced along the seafront into Shoreham.

"Do you reckon he's in there?" Abby asked as she gripped the door handle. The comms from the observation vehicle was being relayed over the radio.

Scott grimaced. Travelling at such speed and in such close proximity to the vehicles in front and behind, he struggled to look at Abby. "I hope so. It's a gamble, but equally, we didn't have time to set up an obs, especially if Sam Tearl is in there. If he got wind of us snooping around, he could be gone long before we get there."

The vehicles killed their sirens and lights long before they travelled down Marlborough Road in Lancing. The observation vehicle identified the exact unit, and the four vehicles pulled up outside. Vehicle doors were opened and closed quietly, and a dozen officers gathered outside the shuttering.

Berry for a change had done as she was told; she stayed back by the cars as an observer.

The first officers on the scene had confirmed that as well as the shuttering to the front, there was also a side access door. Scott instructed Mike and Helen together with two uniformed officers from the entry team to go in via the side door.

With all officers in position, they fell silent. Everyone waited on Scott's command. He leant his ear against the shuttering to see if he could hear anything, but all sounded quiet. He checked his watch and counted down from five to one silently before he gave the tactical entry team the nod to go, go, go.

The chunky padlock offered little resistance for the large bolt croppers. With a swift snap it was easily discarded, and within seconds the shuttering was rolled up, flooding the dark interior with brilliant sunshine.

Scott and the team raced in. Scott's heart was pounding, his mouth parched dry.

They screamed, "Police, stay where you are!"

The noise of their voices and heavy footsteps was matched in equal proportion by the bark from the black German shepherd K9 that stood at the entrance, straining on the leash. He had reared up onto his hind legs, his white teeth showing.

Police flashlights peppered the darkest corners of the workshop with light. The smell of engineering oil hung in the air. Evidence of its use was clear from the black, greasy residue that stuck to shoes.

Scott tried the light switches, but the power had been disconnected. However, he noticed a car battery that had been attached to some lights to provide crude temporary lighting.

Raj and Abby had made their way over to the only furniture in the room. A table with an office chair was positioned in front of a full-length mirror. On the desk were a closed laptop and a camcorder. An empty bottle of red wine and a used glass were perched on the corner of the desk.

Mike and Helen had stormed through the side access only to find themselves in front of a set of stairs that led up to several empty rooms. A damp musty space awaited them that was too dark to see much. The windows had been sealed on the outside with steel shuttering to stop unwelcome visitors. In one room, their torches picked out a solitary desk and chair in one corner; the floor was strewn with paper.

Mike moved around the upper floor using the same stealth as he had been trained to in the army. His footsteps were measured, light, and silent as he checked from left to right. One hand rested on the grip of the taser, ready to be drawn at the slightest threat.

Scott felt his heart was about to burst out of his chest from the adrenaline. He waited for the word from his team.

"Clear," Mike said from the upper floor.

The other officers continued to investigate the remainder of the large unit. Scott watched as the K9 dragged his handler over to a particular section of the unit. He gave a nod to the handler, who let the dog off the leash. The dog raced off to a darkened corner where flattened cardboard boxes were stacked neatly. He buried his nose in the bottom of the pile before taking a step back and barking to alert his handler.

"Good boy. Guv, we have something here."

Scott joined the officer, and together they began to remove the boxes. They revealed a large steel box approximately five feet long set against the wall. They exchanged nervous glances, unsure of its contents. There was always a risk of a booby trap, as Mike had pointed out from his days in the army. Every corner, every room, and every street presented a threat to life. A sniper, an IED, or a child suicide bomber were daily threats.

But the risk was minimal, in Scott's opinion. He grabbed the clasp and lifted the lid as Raj and Abby looked on.

A mixture of fear and relief washed over him as he discovered a female. Scott leant in to feel for a pulse on her wrist. He gave a relieved nod to confirm she was alive.

"Call for an ambulance," Scott barked. "And give me a jacket and something to cut these ties... Get her some water now. Sam? Sam, I'm Detective Inspector Baker from Brighton CID. You're safe now."

Sam remained unresponsive.

The dog pulled his handler towards the back of the unit. "Guv, Merlin has picked up another scent."

"Abby, you stay with her until the ambulance arrives. Raj, you're with me," Scott instructed with urgency in his voice.

The dog handler had already disappeared through the back door, which led down some darkened steps into the basement, swiftly followed by Mike. Scott had only reached the top of the stairs when he heard the officer shout, "Police, stay where you are!"

A cacophony of noise echoed up the narrow staircase as the officer's voice was drowned out by the barking. Scott and Raj quickened their pace, taking two steps at a time. They were followed by two other uniformed officers.

The stairs led into a small dark, dank room with bare, darkened brick walls and a dusty concrete floor. A single camping light sat on a small desk. It offered nothing more than a yellow, luminous glow, which cast dancing shadows of the officers as they manoeuvred around the space.

Brian Hopper sat on a small stool, with one leg crossed over the other and his hands resting on his knees. Mike grabbed the man by his shoulders and threw him to the floor, securing him with handcuffs.

"Brian Hopper?" Scott asked, bending over to examine the man's face.

Brian Hopper greeted him with a smile. "Yes. You moved quicker than I expected."

"Get him out of here, Mike!" Scott growled as the other officers retreated up the stairs.

Hopper offered some resistance, but not enough to bother Mike as he was jostled up the stairs.

Hopper protested and pleaded as he was led away. "But you don't understand, I can't leave Sally alone. She won't be able to cope without me. She needs me to look after her. Can you give me your assurance that you will look after her safely?"

Scott repeated, "Get him out of my sight, Mike."

57

Workers from the other units had filed out on to the road or were peering through their windows to check out the commotion. Scott could see several people taking pictures and videos of the scene as they laughed and joked.

Paramedics had arrived whilst Scott was downstairs and had administered first aid to stabilise Sam's condition. He felt a sigh of relief as he stood outside the unit. The tension that had stiffened his shoulders began to ease off. An overwhelming sense of tiredness washed over him as he leant against the wall.

The team were busy recalling the series of events that had led up to the result. He could see the relief on their faces as they smiled and puffed out their cheeks. In all the commotion, he'd forgotten about Berry, who stood across the street, talking in hushed tones on her phone. He didn't care what she did. She had nothing to throw at him, and she knew it.

"Who is the DCI talking to?" Abby asked.

Scott shrugged. "Your guess is as good as mine. She's

probably feeding back to Meadows about what a fantastic job she's done."

"And that doesn't bother you?"

"Not anymore. Trust me, she'll be running back to Essex before the shit hits the fan."

Abby narrowed her eyes at Scott, searching for a further explanation, but before he could offer her one, an officer urgently requested Scott's attendance.

Scott tensed again. *What have they found?*

He and Abby followed the officer back down into the basement, where a large police torch cast a bright glow on the gloomy space. Uniformed officers had discovered a second box buried into a makeshift hole in the floor covered by a board and then camouflaged with sand. It was identical in nature to the one they had discovered upstairs.

Skeletal remains had been discovered. The bones had been neatly laid out. A blouse and skirt had been positioned over the remains. A cup and saucer with what appeared to be tea and a few biscuits sat beside the box. Her copper-tinted hair was the only clue to her identity. In a macabre way, the skeleton appeared to be smiling at them.

58

There had been a collective sigh of relief following the capture of Brian Hopper and the safe return of Sam Tearl. The student would be under observation and assessment by psychologists. Scott knew that her life would never be the same, and that she would need weeks and perhaps months of counselling to come to terms with the trauma she had experienced.

He felt emotionally and physically drained in the hours and days following Hopper's arrest. The result had reflected well on Scott's team and that of Sussex Police, which CC Lennon had made a point of highlighting in the press conference that followed.

Forensics were in the final stages of their examination of the skeletal remains. Hair fibre analysis confirmed that the remains belonged to Sally Martin. During his interview, Hopper had confirmed that he had attacked Sally Martin because she had refused his advances. He'd also forced Sally to reveal her PIN for her bank card. Thinking it would defuse the situation, she'd given him the details. Sally had fought back and tried to escape, but a savage act of brutality had ended her life in her office. Hopper was in love with Sally and, believing she was feigning death, had taken her body.

Cara squeezed Scott's hand as they sat in his car by the seafront and watched the waves rolling hypnotically towards the shore. They were mesmerised as one wave after another formed an orderly queue before exploding onto the beach.

"I'm glad I've got you all to myself," Cara said. "I don't care what you say, you and I are going online this afternoon, and we're booking a holiday. I don't care where we go, but we're going tomorrow." She added, "I've actually got a friend who's got a family apartment in Spain. It's really quiet, no tourists, and it's such a beautiful little town where we can walk along the beach and feel the sand in our toes and dine on freshly caught fish. I've got the keys already, so what do you think?"

Scott laughed. "I'm sold. I'm sure Abby can hold the fort whilst I'm away."

There was a comfortable silence between them before Cara continued, "Why did he do it?"

"Hopper?"

"Yes."

"He was a manic schizophrenic with bipolar. He'd developed an obsession with redheads after seeing Sally Martin. He was so twisted that the more he saw her, the more he believed that she wanted to see him. He fell in love with her and couldn't bear to be apart from her. The only problem was, she wanted to see him in a professional capacity. In his warped little mind, he thought she was genuinely interested in him. She would get him to talk about his past, his aspirations, getting better, and he took that as a sign that she wanted to find out more about him because she was keen on him."

"And he killed her because of that?"

"Sort of. When she felt he was becoming emotionally attached and dependent upon her, she wanted to terminate their sessions and refer him to a different psychiatrist. That pushed him over the edge. He tried to grab her to tell her how much he loved her, but she pushed him off. And that's when he attacked her." Scott sighed as he thought about the situation Sally had found herself in. "He squirrelled her body away because in his mind he believed that she was still alive and asleep. He was so mentally disturbed that it's shocking. He used to take her a cup of tea and some biscuits every day. But he believed she was off her food and feeling unwell, because she never touched anything."

Cara shook her head in shock. "That's proper messed up."

Scott agreed. "He stopped taking his medication a long time ago and became further unstable and irrational. For reasons he can't explain, he ended up in Sussex. He tried to get meds from the hospital to drug the women he kidnapped, but each time they became suspicious, he legged it, and as a result, his episodes became erratic, frequent and more disturbing. Kidnapping redheads was his way of proving to Sally that he was attractive to other women, namely redheads. He was trying to make her jealous. Over time his obsession grew."

"Well, he's a very sick man. Let's hope he gets put away for a very long time."

Scott nodded and blew out his cheeks in relief as he gazed out towards the sea. Not only had he cracked the case, but his team had come through safely, plus he had dispatched Berry.

Much to Meadows's and Abby's surprise, Berry had abruptly departed for Essex. In the hours following Hopper's arrest, Abby had noticed Berry's absence and had pressed Scott for an explanation.

Scott had explained to Meadows that he'd made discreet enquiries with a few contacts he still had within Essex Police. It transpired that Berry's investigation into Sally Martin's disappearance had been flawed. For whatever reason, they had failed to do thorough checks on Sally's bank account.

At the time, the bank manager had noticed large daily withdrawals from her account that continued for over two months. He'd been surprised that the police hadn't contacted him after her disappearance despite expressing his concerns to the SIO that Sally wasn't replying to his calls or letters.

The money had allowed Hopper to stay under the radar and pay for everything in cash over the past few years and go on to commit further murders.

That was the ace up his sleeve Scott had needed to push Berry into a corner.

"And Berry. She disappeared sharpish," Cara pointed out.

"Her mismanagement of the Sally Martin case has indirectly led to the death of two female students and the abduction of another on our patch. They are deaths that could have been avoided if Berry had acted appropriately. That discovery would leave Berry with lots of questions to answer when the DPS and IOPC begin their investigations into the handling of the Sally Martin case."

"I'm proud of you, Scottie," Cara whispered and squeezed his hand.

"Thanks," he replied as he gazed at her. "I'm glad it's over. And thank you for your support and, well, just being there for me all the time. I don't know about you, but I'm ready for an early night."

Cara checked the time on her phone and furrowed her brow. "It's just gone three p.m...."

"And?" Scott replied with a grin as he started the car.

WE HOPE YOU ENJOYED THIS BOOK

If you could spend a moment to write an honest review on Amazon, no matter how short, we would be extremely grateful. They really do help readers discover new authors.

ALSO BY JAY NADAL

TIME TO DIE

(Book 1 in the DI Scott Baker series)

THE STOLEN GIRLS

(Book 2 in the DI Scott Baker series)

ONE DEADLY LESSON

(Book 3 in the DI Scott Baker series)

IN PLAIN SIGHT

(Book 4 in the DI Scott Baker series)

Printed in Great Britain
by Amazon

19184848R00171